Life's
Toolbox

Firsts

Life's
Toolbox

experience and wisdom
gained through
some of life's

Firsts

Edited by Sandra Joy
Contributions by:

Black Crow Walking ~ ~ Bronwyn MacRitchie
Diana Souter ~ Geoff Gibbson ~ George Graves
George Haith ~ Jan Mitchell ~ John Franks
Judy Turner ~ Kate Mannell ~ Lorraine James
Maggie Rose Carr ~ Margaret Lock
Meg Boland ~ Pat Allen ~ Pat Fern
Patricia Ruell ~ Sandra Joy ~ Tony Lang

KANI CONSULTANTS
Publishing Services

Title: Life's Toolbox / Firsts

First published in 2023 by Kani Consultants, Newcastle, Australia.

A catalogue record for this work is available from the National Library of Australia

Edited by Sandra Boyd

Copyedited by Shannon Benton

First printed by Lightning Source

ISBN: 978-0-6450773-1-5 Life's Toolbox / Firsts

Also available:

978-0-6450773-2-2 Life's Toolbox / Pets and Pests

978-0-6450773-3-9 Life's Toolbox / Silent Train Wrecks

Foreword

These anthologies are dedicated to all writers - past, present and future; emerging and experienced; creators of all genres and enjoyment. Keep up the great work!

The idea for these publications was born from the excitement of watching new writers see their work in print for the first time. I want to spread the joy of experiencing, "It's a real book!"

In this day of fake news, I also want readers to know whether the stories they read are true stories, inspired by true stories, or total fiction.

At the end of the book is a place for you to record some of your firsts. I hope the stories and poems in this book inspire you to try some more new experiences. *Perhaps you can write about them for a future edition*. Then there is a place for you to write your thoughts about the book before you pass it on to someone else.

I wish to thank the brilliant artists who added life to this book: Jessica Hartman and Lea Dee for the artwork and cover design and John Franks for supplying your own photos – thank you for being willing to share such personal images.

Of course, anthologies would not exist without the talented and diverse range of authors whose talents I hold in high esteem.

Very little copyediting was needed, but even the minutest of improvements were picked up by

Shannon Benton – thank you for helping to make us all look good.

Thank you to all contributors for having the patience of Job, and waiting for me to finish my university degree before finding the time to finish publishing your stories.

Finally, to you, the reader: thank you for supporting this project, the authors and the Australian literary industry. I hope you enjoy the contents of these pages.

Sandi

Contents

Part 1:

FIRST

Relationships

Inspired

Rewriting a Life

Jan Mitchell

Lydia nearly went home again. She hadn't brought paper and pen. *Stupid really, since it was a writing group!*

"Today's topic is 'survival'", June, the group leader announced. "You have twenty minutes to write and then we'll hear your stories."

Twelve heads bowed over their notepads. Some members of the group frowned, puzzled or sucked the ends of their pens while others scribbled furiously.

Lydia could hear the clock ticking. It reverberated loudly around the room that was otherwise, only filled with the sounds of breathing and the flow of ballpoint pens over paper. Occasionally, someone sighed and scratched out a word or two that disappointed them.

This was Lydia's first attendance at a writing group. She was unsure of what this exercise was about – of what was expected. The lady next to her – Josie – gave her some paper, and the woman across the other side of the table lent her a pen. Charlotte was on her name badge.

An idea popped into Lydia's head and she began to write, more ideas flowing as she settled in. She wrote about moving from Hong Kong to Sydney during the late 1990s when the Chinese took control of the island. She had been born there, educated and married there. Unlike her, Peter was Anglo. They'd worked in the same company.

When Peter was transferred to Sydney, it was the first time she had walked on foreign soil. Cruelly, the company hadn't given her a transfer. Now that she and Peter were retired, they had decided to move again, north from the big city to live out their final years beside the lake, where Peter could indulge himself with his new boat and go out fishing.

At first, Lydia was at a loss with how to fill her time. Her neighbours rushed off to work every morning and she was dreadfully lonely without Peter. Friends she and Peter had made in Sydney had promised to come up to visit. It wasn't a great distance after all. When Lydia phoned to invite them, they had too much happening to be able to visit.

She was desperate to meet new people, intelligent people like herself. Then she saw a notice in the local supermarket about the local writers and decided to go along to see if she would fit in.

Lydia wrote about the depression she suffered after their move to Sydney. She described how she missed the familiar life of the bustling city of Hong Kong; how she frequently found herself wandering the streets of China Town, just to be near other people who looked like her, tears of homesickness streaming down her face.

When Peter found her a secretarial position in the company, she was less miserable. The work was less exciting than her high flying finance job at home. Peter seemed to adapt to their new life so much better than her. And he didn't have to deal with the racism that she felt every time she shopped.

Now, the move to their dream retirement home had brought back those desperate feelings of being dislocated from all that was familiar. To make matters worse, Peter suffered a stroke moving furniture into their new home and died in the ambulance.

Lydia was still pouring out her misery onto the sheet of paper when June called, "Stop".

Everyone put their pens down. What lovely friendly faces these people had. Most were grey-haired women, one had green dyed hair and of three men, two were bald.

"Who would like to read?" The facilitator looked expectant.

"I will," said Charlotte. Lydia listened to Charlotte's crisp story of a boating accident where, miraculously, after their tinnie sank, three people had managed to scramble over rocks to safety.

"Next," said June, looking pointedly at the man next to Charlotte.

He began to read, stumbling over his own handwriting. He had written about his father surviving when a grenade had dropped into the war-time trench and killed everyone else.

The next member of the group read about her survival giving birth to her first baby alone in the outback. The next piece of writing told of surviving her years at boarding school with a bullying matron.

And so it went on around the group, everyone's story so different from the rest. After the person on Lydia's left had finished reading about her son becoming paraplegic in a car accident, June said,

"Would you like to read, Lydia? Newcomers aren't expected to, but you may."

Lydia blushed at the attention. However, she felt her story was as much a survival story as those others. Maybe people would realise she was lonely and offer friendship?

She swallowed hard and in a very small voice, began. As her story progressed and she gained confidence, people bowed their heads to hide their feelings. Empathy infused the room. When Lydia finished, everyone clapped.

"Well done." "Thank you." "Heartfelt." "How brave you are." Her head swam as the people around her exclaimed.

June clapped her hands. "Thank you for reading today, Lydia. It seems you are looking for a sense of belonging. Maybe you'll find it with our group?"

Lydia felt warmth suffuse her body. Maybe she would find a place here? She decided to return for the next meeting and bring money to join the group. Everyone was different and their stories so diverse, yet they were accepting of each other and, more importantly to Lydia, it seemed they would accept her.

When everyone had finished reading out what they had written, Lydia found she hadn't listened to any more stories. He heart was too full of the friendliness she felt from the people in the room.

As everyone was packing up, Josie approached and invited Lydia to afternoon tea the following week. It was the start of a beautiful friendship, a long association with the writing group and a chance to explore in writing her feelings about calling Australia home.

Source unknown, but I thank whoever first thought of it and all of those who have shared it since.

Attending a wedding for the first time, a little girl whispered to her mother, "Why is the bride dressed in white?"

The mother replied, "Because white is the colour of happiness, and today is the happiest day of her life."

The child thought about this for a moment then said, "So why is the groom wearing black?"

Forbidden Love

Tony Lang

It was love at first sight ... love 'across a crowded room', literally. We belonged to the same organisation, so I saw her only Monday to Friday. I couldn't take my eyes off her.

Unexpectedly, she turned slightly and caught me staring at her. Instead of ignoring me, she smiled back. In the warmth of that smile, I read a promise of things to come.

Her figure was so elegant, her movements as graceful as a swan's. Each time she turned her head, the sunlight streaming through the window highlighted the beauty of the nutbrown hair framing her sweet face. Even the sun seemed besotted. Her name was Heather... such a pretty name.

It took all my strength not to tell the woman I was living with about her, for I loved her too and didn't want to hurt her.

I decided to court my new love gently. I saw her almost daily, noting that she'd bring a sandwich and a piece of fruit to lunch, sit by herself and read. So, by a strange 'coincidence' I was there too and of course in time we began to converse, talking about all sorts of things.

One day as she stood to return to her office, I, greatly daring, slipped my hand into hers. I half-expected her to withdraw hers. She didn't. In fact, she gave my hand a little squeeze. Oh – boundless bliss!

We walked hand in hand back to her office where regretfully I released her.

In the face of such encouragement, my initial hesitation turned to recklessness. I decided to ask her to marry me. Only one woman, whom I'd been with for some years, stood between me and her. I didn't relish the thought of asking 'the other woman' to release me, for I knew she loved me.

I asked her a few weeks later. As she stood to go back to her office, I took her hand in mine and gently kissed it. "Heather, would you ... will you ... marry me?" I knew my face was the colour of tomato soup; my voice a nervous crackle.

I saw at once I'd taken her completely by surprise. She withdrew her hands and smiled; a sad smile, a compassionate smile – a rejecting smile.

"Tony dear, you're the first who has ever asked me, and it hurts me deeply to tell you that I can't ma –"

"Why can't you marry me? I thought you loved me!" My shattered heart released the waters of Burrinjuck. Quietly, she slipped me her handkerchief.

"I do, I do, but it's a different sort of love, Tony dear. Romantic love cannot exist between us. I'm twenty-two, and you're only six. I'm your teacher. I love all of you." She gestured to the class.

She left at the end of that year. It took me a long time to recover – at least a month, and I never did mention the matter to my mother. She probably wouldn't have let me go anyway.

Years later, I met Heather Howie again. She was ninety-two and still retained something of her former loveliness and sweet nature. She'd never married – and to think, she could have had me.

Morgan Has His Turn

Pat Fern

One wet morning in June, Morgan Gilroy decided to have a mid-life crisis. He would be thirty-five in three days. If that wasn't the middle of life, what was?

His parents had been law abiding to a fault. They both relinquished their hold on life a few weeks past their respective seventieth birthdays. Three score years and ten they were allowed, and three score years and ten they took.

He looked round the beige walled office, hating it. He loathed the battered timber veneer desk with the accompanying crippling chair that had been his for eighteen years. He hated the large computer monitor that had commanded his reluctant attention for ten of those years.

He regarded the people who were still strangers, even after working together for so long. They were hidden behind their screens. Morgan had no idea what they looked like. The door was behind him so he didn't see them come and go. He vaguely saw the two men and one woman who shared his front row. They never spoke unless they had a work-related query. He knew their names from the identity badges they were compelled to wear. Surnames only. Typical of this horrible firm.

They were colleagues, not friends.

"Enough." Morgan banged his hand on his desk as hard as he could. The hum of a busy office stopped. In the silence, faces turned this way and that looking for the source of disruption.

Company policy discouraged socialising in working hours. Most of their employees lived in far-flung suburbs so they never met by accident at weekends. They spun round each other like orbiting planets with as little contact as necessary to do the job, nothing more. Morgan knew most of them had families, hobbies and lives away from the firm of Whitford Grange and Sons Pty Ltd, who paid their wages each month. Morgan had nobody. Picking up his briefcase, he left the office without a backward glance, only pausing to take his overcoat from its peg.

He paused again to take stock when he reached the busy street, absent mindedly sucking his hand where he hit the desk. How did one have a mid-life crisis? He heard stories of men discarding wives for younger women. He wasn't married. He heard of old family cars being traded in for high powered sports models. Not only did Morgan not own a car, he couldn't drive.

What a pathetic apology for a man I am. I don't even have anything to give up.

His usual bus stop beckoned. How many hours of his life had he spent waiting for the bus to Hemel Hempstead?

"Damn it, I'll walk." A twenty-minute bus ride took at least two hours on foot. He didn't mind, it was a lovely day in spite of the cold rain. He strolled along familiar streets enjoying the feeling of not having to be anywhere.

He looked in a smart menswear shop marveling at the latest fashions.

He assessed his wardrobe. He owned two smart pinstriped business suits, one navy, one dark grey, each with its matching tie. Five white business shirts, two white sports shirts, one pair of casual trousers – grey. Seven pairs of socks, some grey, some blue, one pair of black oxfords, one pair of black loafers. There was the long dark blue overcoat he was wearing now. He had very few casual clothes, he didn't need them.

Weekends were spent tending the large, handsome house with its extensive garden that he inherited from his parents. On Saturday mornings he pushed a trolley round Sainsbury's wearing his tailored casual trousers with a sports shirt. If it was cold, he also wore his blue knitted jumper or the brown checked sports jacket with leather patches on the elbows that had been his father's. It was older than he was.

He lived in the house where he was born. He seldom traveled outside Hertfordshire except for annual holidays in Ramsgate. Always the same place. He had never seen any of the rest of the United Kingdom. His brown, wavy hair was cut in the 'short back and sides' style his mother chose when he was two. He even went to the same barber's, for Pete's sake.

Morgan drifted into the menswear shop while he was pondering the dullness of his life. An assistant was politely waiting to enquire, could he help, sir? Yes, mate, you can, I need all the help I can get.

"Yes, I was looking for something – new."

"New? In what way, sir?"

"Something modern, fashionable, cool. Anything that's not grey or blue."

"Ah, yes. I know just what sir wants. May I say it would be a shame to give up blue altogether? It compliments sir's eyes if I may say so?"

"Please stop calling me, sir."

"Yes, sir, of course, sir, I apologise, sir."

Something in his tone made Morgan look at him properly for the first time. He saw a grey haired, dapper man with penetrating pale blue eyes that were twinkling at him while a grin hovered at the corners of his mouth. There was an expression in those eyes that Morgan couldn't place. They knew him, through and through.

"I think you would look very handsome in a pair of our designer jeans, Mr. Gilroy. We also have some very smart knitted cotton shirts that will be ideal for summer."

"How do you know my name?" His startled question went unanswered as the assistant bustled over to a rack. He ran an expert eye over Morgan before selecting three pairs of jeans in varying shades of denim.

"You'll find these will fit you perfectly, Morgan."

Hours later, Morgan emerged laden with bags containing jeans, trousers and shirts with matching accessories. His wallet and his heart were both considerably lighter. He'd had a wonderful time. He couldn't believe the good-looking young man in the shop mirrors was stuffy Morgan Gilroy.

He realised the helpful grey-haired assistant never answered his questions. He still had no idea how the man knew his name. It was odd that he didn't care. He'd been drawn out with the skill of a psychiatrist combined mind-reader. Never before had he talked about himself so openly, even to his parents. Especially to his parents.

He knew they loved him as much as he loved them. They would have been horrified to the depths of their conservative souls if they had known the ambitions and dreams that he harboured under his quiet, obedient exterior.

When he left school, his father found him a job at the import and export company where he had worked for forty-five years.

"Nothing like a nice secure office job to set you up for life just as it has me. Look at the nice house it brought us. We have enough to live on in our old age and leave you a good bit." Morgan noticed that 'nice' was his father's favourite word.

His parents smiled indulgently when Morgan tried to point out that he didn't want security. Before he knew it, he was established at the battered desk where he was to spend the next eighteen years. His dreams of becoming a pilot were crushed under the weight of accounts, in, out and pending.

"Why don't you become a pilot, you're still young? Thirty-five is no age at all."

When the assistant put it like that, Morgan could see himself at the controls of a 747, or even one of the new air buses. Captain Morgan Gilroy. How did the man know his age? He hadn't mentioned his ambitions to be a pilot either.

"Why shouldn't you have a girlfriend, you have everything to offer?"

Morgan visualised women queuing round the block to become Mrs. Morgan Gilroy.

"There is a woman for you. She's been near to you for years." How could he know where near to Morgan would be?

"Take driving lessons, buy a car, have fun."

Dashing Morgan Gilroy waved from his bright red sports car. There was the smart family car for his three, beautiful children. His gorgeous wife would drive them to school. He would drive it when they went on family outings.

Talking in the shop made everything possible. He turned back to thank the man who opened up a lifetime of possibilities. He couldn't see the shop. Surely, he hadn't walked so far, he'd lost sight of it. Strangely, it no longer mattered. When he needed more clothes, it would be there. He was as certain of that as he was of his own name.

He determined that he would have his turn at life. He passed a driving school, then backtracked and entered. He came out with an appointment for the next Wednesday. He was on his way. When he saw a bus for Hemel Hempstead standing at a stop, he ran for it. It was too late now to arrive home in daylight with his unwieldy parcels. It was Friday. Adventures could wait until the next day.

He was startled when the phone rang that evening. It seldom rang. He sometimes wondered why he had one.

He was even more surprised at hearing a female voice.

"Hi Morgan, it's Catherine Menzies. Call me Cathie. I thought I'd ring and tell you what a stir you caused at work. It was great. We all started talking after you went. Sir wasn't thrilled."

Morgan imagined his boss's sour expression above the well-cut dark suit. No, Mr. Bromhedge would not be pleased.

"Do I know you?"

"Miss Menzies, four desks across in front of the ratty rubber plant. We don't have much to do with each other. I work on the Browning account."

Morgan recalled a quiet girl, usually wearing a grey or beige business suit matched with high-necked white or cream blouses. Blondish hair dragged back in a neat roll. Discreet, expertly applied make up.

"Sorry, of course I know you. It was the Cathie that threw me. What did Sir say? I bet he fired me on the spot." There was a delighted giggle.

"He tried. When he realised it was too late, he threw one of his tantrums. We've never had so much fun at work. We all know each other's Christian names now. In future we are going to talk to each other whatever the company says. I sneaked a look in your file to find your Christian name, address and phone number. I only live a couple of roads away from you."

"I've never seen you on the bus."

"I drive." This girl drove. Morgan didn't have the courage to admit he was about to have his first driving lesson.

"Morgan, I was wondering, could we go out tomorrow? We could have a picnic in St Albans Park. I'll pick you up."

Morgan blushed. She knew he couldn't drive.

"That would be great. My car is in for repairs." He could hear the lie in his voice. Cathie had to be aware of it.

When he answered the door the next morning, Morgan was transfixed by the vision on his front path. Glowing in a low-cut yellow dress, golden hair flowing round perfect tanned shoulders, Cathie smiled.

Morgan fell in love. He dragged his eyes away from her magnificent cleavage. A vagrant breeze blew her full skirt to reveal smooth brown legs that went up for ever.

"Aren't you going to say something," Cathie asked. Morgan closed his mouth with an effort. Cathie, well aware of the turmoil she caused kissed him full on the lips. "I've always wondered what kissing you would be like. Lovely." She kissed him again.

The day in St Albans Park was perfect. They explored majestic St Albans Abbey, marveling at the long dead workmen who could conceive and build such a structure without modern machinery. Hand in hand they wandered across the playing fields to the Verulamium Museum. Morgan held her, patting her back awkwardly as she wept for the skeletons displayed with so little dignity. She was particularly affected by the new born babies who never had the chance to live. Together they marveled at the Roman hypocaust, so perfectly preserved after thousands of years.

Cathie prepared a delicious picnic, smiling at Morgan's praise.

"Of course, I'm a fantastic cook. I can do all sorts of wonderful things."

"I have a confession," he couldn't let a lie come between them. "I don't have a car. I can't drive yet. I'm having my first lesson on Wednesday."

"I knew that. I like a bit of male pride. When you're ready, you can practice in my car when we go out."

It took Morgan a mere month to pass his driving test. His instructor told him he was a pleasure to teach, and that he had an aptitude for driving. He and Cathie spent a happy day looking at cars before Morgan became the proud owner of a brand-new silver Ford.

Encouraged by his driving success, he took flying lessons. His excellent mathematics found a worthy outlet. Soaring through the sky totally in charge of the Cessna, he knew that for the first time in his life he was in his true element. He passed the written examinations with ease and put in the required flying hours to be granted his licence.

He visited the menswear shop many times during those happy months. He commented to the grey-haired assistant that it was strange that sometimes the shop seemed not to be there.

"Our ladies and gentlemen can always find us when they need us."

Morgan's curiosity always faded when he tried to ask a question. The assistant admitted his name was Michael. He listened smiling as Morgan told him about his latest accomplishments.

Morgan's wardrobe grew in quantity and style. When he proudly introduced Cathie, Michael didn't quite say "I told you so." Morgan could see it in Michael's eyes while it hovered on his lips. He admired his friend's self-restraint for it was a very near thing.

Morgan proposed to Cathie on the day he was accepted as a pilot with an airline that flew passengers all over the British Isles. Over a celebratory dinner in a small, romantic restaurant by the River Thames where the full moon silvered the water, Morgan ignored the stares of the other diners as he went down on one knee.

"Catherine Menzies, I have loved you since the first time I saw you on my front door step. Darling Cathie, will you do me the honour of becoming my wife?"

"Yes, yes, a thousand times, yes." She squealed with delight when he put the sapphire and diamond ring on her finger. "How did you know I love sapphires?"

"You told me." He didn't add that Michael knew her ring size, although he couldn't work out how. By then Morgan had such faith in Michael's judgment that he accepted every word he said as gospel. Once he would have cringed with embarrassment when the entire restaurant broke into applause.

Captain Morgan Gilroy simply laughed then took Cathie by the hand while bowing left and right. He beckoned the waiter, grandly ordering champagne for everyone, including the staff.

"A toast everyone, to Catherine, my future wife."

A few days later Cathie looked round Morgan's home.

"It's a great house, darling, I would love to live here … but, when was it last redecorated?"

"Not in my lifetime." Morgan looked at the ugly wallpaper, old fashioned furniture and fittings. It was straight out of the forties.

"You have a free hand. We'll go shopping tomorrow."

The house blossomed under Cathie's expert hand. The Salvation Army took the furniture. Light, bright paint replaced the wallpaper Morgan gleefully peeled from the walls. His home, their home, became everything he ever dreamed it could be.

He was beginning to have suspicions about Michael and his shop. He needed a guardian angel. Did he have one?

Although there was no doubt there were other customers visiting Michael's shop, he never saw anybody else while he was there. It was floating in time and space waiting for lost souls to pass by. Or did it seek them out? Morgan accepted that he would never know. He was content.

Morgan never imagined a wedding day would ever come into his proscribed, friendless existence.

He stood at the alter watching his bride coming toward him radiant in elegant, form fitting satin followed by four bridesmaids who seemed a pale blue extension of her long, graceful train. Thinking back to the day he thumped his desk; Morgan considered his mid-life crisis to be extremely satisfactory. Well worth a bruised hand. His best man winked at him.

"I told you so." said Michael.

The Locket

Margaret Lock

Most mornings, I'd see him standing outside the tiny real estate office waiting for his lift to work. After stopping to buy a newspaper at the general store, I'd pass him down the track to the station, pretending I hadn't noticed him.

John, dark-haired, tall and well-built, played for the local football team and was a member of the fire brigade. After school one day, I talked my sisters, Jenny and Anne, into accompanying me to footy practise.

Just before the lads finished practise, I overheard a young player teasing John. "There's your girlfriend over there", he laughed, to which John playfully clouted him across the ear.

After footy practise, I hung around with Jenny and Anne and then John came over to say hello. After my sisters turned for home, we headed down the track leading to the main road. Before reaching Dad's mixed business on the corner, John asked if I'd go to the dance with him on Saturday fortnight. My heart fluttered as I replied, "Yes" and I noticed his face was beaming.

That week, John came into the shop after work and asked if I'd like to go to the pictures. Come Saturday night, we headed to the local hall with my sisters trailing behind us. After watching the eye-opening 'Jailhouse Rock', Jenny and Anne tagged behind, yet again, as John and I walked hand in hand along the footpath. He wisely chose to ignore them, but I cringed whenever they giggled and made comments like, "Look at them holding hands."

John kept himself busy working at Smythe's supermarket in Northridge, a short train ride away. He also helped support his deserted mother who struggled to raise his four younger siblings. Footy practise and fire drill also demanded much of his time, so he needed to be ready and available when needed.

Late one evening, John came to visit, just as my family were heading off to bed. Sitting on the old club sofa, we decided to watch an old movie and during an ad break John turned and grinned, reaching for my hand. Smiling uncertainly, I placed my right elbow on the arm of the sofa, resting my chin on my right hand while pretending I was focused on the movie. Instinctively, John reached over and grabbed my spare hand, leaving me vulnerable and slightly ill at ease.

By the time the movie finished it was late, so when he rose to leave I followed him to the back door. Then, turning around, he said in a low voice that he loved me. He wore a funny, shy smile when he said those words, and I couldn't believe my ears. I'd only been out with him once, and this was totally unexpected. All I knew was, my heart was thumping hard in my chest and my face froze as I meekly said goodnight, watching in disbelief as he headed off home.

I knew for certain that I wasn't anywhere near ready to hear those words. I wasn't quite fifteen, though it was true I'd been infatuated with him for months. He was seventeen and must have been ready for a more serious relationship, but this was becoming way too scary for me.

One evening that week, while standing behind the shop counter, I nearly jumped out of my skin when the door bell clanged loudly. Then John walked in.

"Happy Birthday," he said in a low, cheerful voice.

Looking down at the counter, I felt myself blushing. I remembered Mum had mentioned my birthday in passing when he'd first visited me at the shop.

"Oh ... thanks," I replied breathlessly, shooting him a smile.

He walked to the end of the counter and followed me through to the kitchen. Standing between the table and the fridge, we stood staring at each other.

Then he took a small wrapped box from his cardigan pocket. Pushing it into my hand, he quietly said, "Here's something for you."

My heart pounded and my face and neck felt hot as I stared down at the small box. Barely breathing, a thought raced through my mind: I hope it's not a ring.

I didn't want to open the gift in front of John, or Dad who was standing at the sink washing the dinner dishes. Turning to speak to John, Dad asked if he'd be available to work in the shop on Sunday afternoon.

While they spoke, I snuck up the steps to my room. Sitting on the side of my bed, my hands shook as I stared down at the small package, wondering, What's inside the box?

I could hear Dad and John talking as I nervously began to unwrap my gift. Then, there it was: a red velvet box. Holding my breath, I tentatively pulled back the lid. Inside, a gold, heart-shaped locket attached to a fine chain lay on a white satin cushion. Carefully removing the locket from the box, I rested it in my palm. The gleaming heart was engraved on the left side with graceful swirls and flowers.

After managing to open the clasp, I found there was enough space inside to hold a tiny photograph. My hands continued to tremble as I attempted to open the catch on the chain, but I couldn't open it on my own. Stepping down into the kitchen, John and Dad stopped talking and stared at me.

"It's lovely ... thank you," I said to John, my eyes briefly meeting his. "Could you do it up for me, please?

John's fingers fumbled with the catch and it seemed ages before he succeeded in fastening it.

"There," he said. "Let's see how it looks."

Still blushing, I turned to face him.

"Perfect!" he smiled. "Now you can wear it to the dance on the weekend."

That Saturday night, John arrived early. After I'd attempted to apply some of Mum's makeup, I checked the long mirror inside my wardrobe door to see if I looked passable before I joined John in the lounge room.

"You look beautiful," he said, standing to greet me. "I really like your dress."

"Thanks," I replied shyly. "Mum gave it to me for my birthday."

"I'm pleased you're wearing the locket."

"Yes." I grinned. "I even managed to do it up this time."

"Good," he laughed. "Well … now you're ready, I s'pose we might as well head off."

After pulling on my white lacy cardigan, I gave John a sheepish grin before grabbing my handbag from the sideboard.

Singing out "Goodbye" to Mum who was in her room, I heard her call, "Come and show me how you look." As I entered the room, she proudly exclaimed, "That dress looks lovely!" The floral and white broderie anglaise creation she'd bought on special at Myer wasn't my choice, but it was the only decent dress I owned. Before John and I left, I also called "Goodbye" to Dad who was in the shop sorting out some stock.

Walking out onto the gravel driveway, John opened the swing gate. After he'd closed it, he reached for my hand and we headed towards the local hall.

Entering the foyer, we heard the band warming up as John took his wallet from his back pocket and pulled out a one pound note.

"Two please," he said to the giggly girls seated behind the table.

Again, he took my hand and we entered the hall where I recognised some high school students and a bunch of locals who frequented Dad's shop. Seated on a bench along the far end of the hall, we looked around at the various groups. Feeling uncomfortably out of place, I found it hard to believe I was really there sitting alongside John.

An old school friend, Gail – wearing a tight short skirt and matching clingy top, with thick, pale makeup covering most of her acne – appeared in her element. She was flirting outrageously with some males hailing from Rainsford Hill where her family ran a huge chook farm.

Finding myself staring at her every now and then, I tried to guess which bloke she was keen on. Resting a hand on her shapely hip, I noticed she was pointing one of her chicken legs towards Albie, a handsome young buck whom I'd heard her discuss in class. I knew he was popular with the girls and Gail's body language made it abundantly clear she was an ardent admirer.

On the stage, the MC introduced himself and welcomed us, with the band striking up a Foxtrot number.

Since John and I had been eyeing off everyone in the hall, we hadn't spoken more than a few words, so when he turned and asked me to dance, my heart almost leapt from my chest.

Noticing I didn't look confident, he leaned in towards me. "We won't have to do much, except shuffle about."

Facing him, I awkwardly placed my hand on his shoulder as he attempted to guide me around the hall. Each time I stood on his feet, I giggled and blushed, constantly finding myself saying "Sorry," to which he just smiled and kept on shuffling. In between dances, he told me again how much he liked my dress, as well as my hair, which made me feel a tad better about my lack of prowess on the dance floor.

As we shuffled out of time to the next number, he laughed. "It's all right," he said. "Maybe we should take some dance lessons."

"Mmm ..." I murmured. "I remember learning The Pride of Erin and The Waltz with Dad years ago, and we had lessons for The Barn Dance and The Evening Three Step before the school social, but I don't know any of these."

I didn't enjoy shuffling around, seeing as most dancers seemed to be doing a good job at fox-trotting and rocking 'n' rolling. Most of the time, John and I seemed to be in the wrong place, causing a few minor collisions. We certainly had a long way to go before we would impress anyone with our dance moves.

At ten o'clock, the MC announced supper was being served in the adjoining room. It was a tight squeeze as around one hundred people headed for the trestle tables laden with sandwiches, savouries and cakes.

"What a feast," John grinned, wide-eyed. "I hope you're hungry."

After filling our paper plates, we edged back to our seats.

Meanwhile, the dance hall was abuzz with conversation and laughter as everyone sat or stood in groups. Then John left to fetch some cups of tea.

A minute later, someone sidled up to me. "How's things going with your fella," a cheeky young voice quipped.

I looked up. It was Alan, the barber's son who occasionally frequented our shop. His family lived over the road and I knew he was one of Gail's ex's.

"Good," I replied shyly, unsure why he was speaking to me. He'd never bothered to acknowledge me in the shop, as he was always busy being smart around his mates. As John returned with our tea, Alan made a quick exit.

"What was *he* doing here?"

"Don't know," I shrugged, carefully taking a cup and saucer from him.

"I didn't know there'd be so many here tonight," John commented. "Almost everyone I know is here … from the fire brigade and the footy …"

"Yes," I nodded. "There're quite a few students here too, and a lot of locals I've served in the shop."

Before the end of the night, we slipped out of the hall and headed home. Walking along, hand-in-hand, I felt on edge, wondering if he'd try and kiss me. After all, a few days earlier he'd said he loved me.

At the swing gate, John unfastened the chain and I walked through. Then, without warning, he turned and wrapped his arms around my shoulders, trying to kiss me as I quickly looked away. After trying again, I gave the same response.

"Why ..." he said, his voice tinged with hurt. "Why won't you let me kiss you?"

I couldn't think of anything to say as we headed for the back door. I had metal braces wired to each of my teeth and felt totally embarrassed now that he wanted to kiss me. However, I couldn't come to grips with reality. It had been all very well to dream about him in romantic situations, but I couldn't tell him my real reasons: my age, my inexperience, my self-consciousness about my braces and my uncertainty about where this could be leading.

It appeared Mum, Dad and my sisters were all in bed and with the place in darkness, John followed me to the door. Trembling, I fumbled to locate the inside light.

In the lounge room, I couldn't look at John. Instead, I sat on the arm of the sofa as he remained standing.

"What have I done wrong?" he pleaded, a puzzled look clouding his face.

"Nothing," I nervously replied. "It was a good night ... thanks."

He stared at the floor.

"I suppose I'd better be off then," he winced.

"Mmm."

"Maybe we could go to the pictures next Saturday," he suggested. Then his voice took on a mocking sound. "We could sit in the back row and you could watch the other couples kissing. You might learn something."

Pulling the chain and locket hard into my neck, I retorted. "Well in that case you can go alone. There're plenty of girls who'd go out with you.

What about that Scottish girl, Heather, who just started working with you?"

"What about her?" he scowled.

"You could take her," I replied, wishing I hadn't mentioned her name.

John never came to the shop again, leaving Dad perplexed when he didn't show up the following afternoon.

"Where's John today?"

"Don't know."

"That's too bad. Did you have a row?"

"Something like that."

One month later, Dad was forced to close the shop as he'd let too many customers tick up their purchases. With a silly laugh, he said my sisters and I must have sent him broke after eating most of the profits. I felt a pang of guilt when he said that, as I knew we'd tucked into far too many milk shakes and lollies than we should have.

A few weeks later, our family moved into a rental house in nearby Wattle Gully. My girlfriend, Denise, told me she'd seen John on the train and he'd asked her out, but she wasn't interested. That put me off him even more.

One of my form members heard I had a boyfriend and asked about him as we waited to go into English class.

"I don't know," I scoffed. "I hate his guts."

A few weeks later, I developed a crush on Donald, a new boy in my English class. He had a sweeping blonde fringe, chiselled tan features and broad shoulders. He was also the newest member of our senior swimming team. When the sports team photos were posted on the notice board, I ordered a copy of his team photo. After collecting it, I took it home and cut out Donald's face, placing it in the locket.

I'd never even spoken to Donald. I only admired him from afar like I'd previously done with John for months before we'd gone out.

Early one evening, before Mum and Dad returned home from work, there were some sharp taps on the front door.

Opening the door, I gasped. It was John. Apparently he'd spoken to a mutual friend on the train one day, and she'd told him our new address.

"Hello," he murmured, looking down. "Can I come in?"

"Er . . . all right," I replied, standing aside.

He followed me into the lounge room where Jenny was watching TV. When she saw John, she blushed and turned away, pretending to watch her show.

I felt uneasy seeing John in our lounge room. His face was expressionless and neither of us had the gumption to start talking. Looking about, I noticed the locket on the mantelpiece and stepped over to pick it up. Opening the clasp, I smirked when I saw Donald's photo.

Looking towards John, I said in a strange, sing-song voice, "This is good for storing a special photo in."

He didn't respond. I don't know why I had to be so cruel, but I felt like taunting him after what Denise told me. Even though I'd felt betrayed, my actions left me feeling sick in the stomach.

After staring at the TV for a couple of tense minutes, John said a curt goodbye and let himself out the front door. I looked at Jenny and pulled a face.

Meanwhile, my heart thumped erratically as I headed to my room. Throwing myself on the bed and burying my face in the pillow, I chastised myself. Why had I said what I said? I knew he'd only asked Denise out because I'd hurt him. John must have still liked me, though, to have gone out of his way to visit, and now I'd blown it forever.

I knew in my heart of hearts that I could never have been the right girl for John. He clearly wanted a serious relationship. After all, he'd be 18 soon and he was looking to find a loving girlfriend.

Over the next few weeks, I continued to check out Donald in class. I wore the locket to school each day, and no one around me would have ever guessed that his face was inside it.

As for John, a few months later he became engaged to that Scottish girl from work. Somehow I felt a great sense of relief. Thank goodness he'd found someone to love. Now I could get on with coming to terms with the fantasies and realities in my life.

More than a Painting

George Graves

Slowly she opened the door. No creak; only the sound of a soft rustle of the autumn leaves on the trees in the front yard. She was surprised her key still worked, after so many years. They said it would, but for some reason, it was still unexpected.

Peering in, she waited a couple of minutes for her eyes to become accustomed to the low light conditions. The room was much the same as she had remembered it, but now it lacked the laughter and happiness she felt so keenly when she was here as a child.

Throwing open a curtain, the dust rose, showing streaks of light from the sun that was almost setting. Even now, she thought of her grandmother as 'Nan'. In the corner stood the piano that she remembered her nan playing, her fingers dancing over the keyboard. Oh, how she enjoyed listening to the music. Sometimes her nan sang along to a tune she knew well.

At other times a piano sonata floated throughout the house. It was probably from the time when she was very young and could only manage something like 'Nan' and 'Pop' that she always used these words.

What wonderful memories she had from her visits on holidays to her grandparents. As both her mother and father were working full time, she spent many a happy time here, just her, with them.

The excitement when Pop gave her a little wooden sailing boat that he had made especially for her. It had a blue hull, a red cabin and two sails and at the front it had a small stick pointing out that her pop had called a bowsprit, when she had asked about it.

They took it down to the nearby lagoon, tied a string to it and let it sail away. And sail it did, so gracefully with a little wave coming from the bow. She was so pleased to have a little boat, one made especially for her, and it sailed beautifully as well as looking so good. At the end of the afternoon, they pulled in the string, wound it up and captured the boat at the water's edge where the sand was soft. She gave a little giggle, remembering how she liked the feel of wriggling her toes in the sand.

They did this many times, and while the boat was sailing, her Pop would tell her about the nearby trees and bushes and the birds that landed on the quiet water or flew overhead. Now and then they would see a little fish dart near the water's edge, where the water was very shallow. He would tell her about it as well. And he taught her to listen to the nearby sounds; the rustle of the wind in the trees, the thunder of the waves breaking on the nearby beach, the shrieks of laughter of some children somewhere, the noise from an aeroplane carrying people away on holidays and in the distance, the harsh jarring noise of trucks and cars on the motorway.

But it was not all about learning. Often, they would just sit beside each other, watching the little boat bobbing on the waves, and looking at the colour of the sky during another golden sunset. It was undoubtedly this time with her Pop that led to her appreciation and love of nature as an adult.

What did she remember of her Pop? She remembered the things they did together, but what was he like? Strangely, the memories were not so clear. He had always seemed old to her, with his grey beard streaked with white. And his hair was grey also, with lots of white in it. Not that she could see much of it when they went out as he always seemed to wear his old broad-brimmed fishing hat. He was gentle and spoke softly to her and she so loved him.

A couple of times he and Nan had words about something she knew nothing about or did not understand and he would disappear to his shed. Sometime later he would reappear and give Nan a hug. Perhaps, as she knew now, it wasn't the best way of sorting out an argument but it seemed to work for them.

Her grandparents had both now sadly passed away and her parents had asked her if she would like something from the house. "Probably not", she had replied. The most valuable thing was the memories of the times she had with them.

She had gone to university and then went to live overseas for several years, and during that time, had written lots of letters to them, so she had kept close to them. She smiled as she remembered her nan's attempts at that newfangled thing called email. Sometimes she received one that just said: *letter going*. And the handwritten one would arrive, sometimes a couple of weeks later, in her letterbox.

Looking around the room, almost hidden behind the lounge, she noticed a painting that had fallen from the wall. Picking it up and wiping the dust from the glass, she realised she did not recognise it.   It had not been there when she was a child.

Holding it at arm's length, she looked at it. It was like a French impressionist style. Something like a Renoir. Not all the detail was there, but enough to convey the scene. It was a view of a street, probably in Paris.

On the sides of the street there were cafes, with people sitting around tables on the footpaths, enjoying their food and drinks.

To the left, a man and a woman sat facing each other. She was wearing an elegant long light cream coloured dress, with short sleeves that puffed out, trimmed with lace.

Interestingly, for that time, the dress came up to her neck, again with lace around it, and with lace across her bodice. She was also wearing a little hat. Well, some may call it a hat, but it looked like a flat section of lace, with a small flower, worn towards the side of her head. Her hair was auburn, curly with locks cascading over one of her shoulders and down her back. She looked to be in her young twenties, fairly slender, and was looking intently at her friend. She was sitting forward, with her hands on the table, one covered by one of her friend's hands. He appeared to be dressed in a mid-blue suit. Not much could be seen of him, as he was facing away, towards his friend. His hat sat on the table, near their hands.

It looked to be late in the afternoon. The gas lamps had already been lit and there were streaks of light reflecting in the puddles of water on the road. It had been raining previously and the mist still hung around the gas lamps, creating a softness to the scene.

In the distance, a carriage was coming, the driver with the reins in one hand, intent on the path the horse was taking. The street was dimpled in places where the cobblestones were worn. There were some other people strolling along the street and some were looking in the widows, pointing out something to their companion. All the people in the painting appeared to be talking or listening to someone else. It was as though the artist had captured the scene with no one noticing him at all.

Except for one person.

In the middle of the road, looking up, directly at the artist, stood a small boy. She could see his eyes looking straight at her. He was not dressed very well. His jacket was dirty, his trousers had a hole in one knee and his bare feet were half covered by a puddle. He had one arm outstretched, the other down beside him.

The painting captured her attention. She put it down on the lounge, resting it back on the cushions, and looked at it again, particularly at the figure of the small boy. His eyes seemed to plead: "Take me away from all this."

Am I like this little boy, she thought? *Do I want a bit of help when I am not coping?*

Would I have liked for someone to come and take me away from a situation I have been in? Well, when I was away at uni and I had the flu, I would have liked my mum to come and give me a hug and make some food for me. That would have been so good. But that was different. Usually I look after myself well, I do things and am not too worried by changes.

Now, my best friend, Katrina, whom I have known from kindergarten, is a bit like that boy, not that I would ever tell her. She stayed in the town when I went to the city. She is still there in the place where she is unexcited by her job.

And there are few, or is that no, young available men there. She is such a great friend and we talk to each other so often but, at times, she seems to want to be taken away from it all, without her doing anything about it.

Why am I in such a contemplative mood today? I suppose it's coming back to this house again, and all the memories that have been woken up. The times when I was a little girl and life seemed so wonderful and I didn't need to plan for the next weekend because the next weekend seemed so far away.

Yes, life is quite wonderful now. I don't have the pressure of exams in a month's time any more. And thinking of wonderful ... well, Mark is. He's not perfect but wonderful seems to fit. It is so good to see him. We enjoy doing things together, like going on a bushwalk or out to the movies or visiting friends. However, the best times are when I go to his place and we just listen to music together. That is so good. All the trivia of life seems to fade away then.

How hard it must be for some people who do not enjoy their life and find it impossible to change it. Elderly, lonely people who find it so hard to get out except for some food shopping. People in relationships where the love has faded, or worse, become changed due to violence. The chap she had seen on the bench by the park, as she walked to the house.

She looked at the picture again and studied the little boy. He is captive to the canvas. He is completely dependent on someone else coming to wipe the dust off his face and on the painting being hung on the wall so he can be seen again.

We are different. We can make a difference to ourselves but sometimes it may seem so hard. For some people it really is so difficult.

We are more than the little boy. He is captive; we have choices. We can help others with some small thing and perhaps sometimes bring a smile to another's face.

The world has so much to see, to read about, to experience, even to be seen on TV, that it is a shame if we chose to do only the mundane.

Where are all these thoughts coming from, she thought? *This is not like me. Well, that is not quite true. I am a bit contemplative, well, a wee bit anyway, now and then,* she conceded with some embarrassment.

Looking around the room, she noticed the shadows lengthening. She had better be going soon. Yes, she would accept something from the house. If the painting had not been already claimed by anyone else, she would like to have it.

However, the painting had already claimed her, so she would like to accept it.

French Doors
and Red Curls

Black Crow Walking

French doors open onto a cacophony of
bleeding heart vines
covered in spring flowers,
drowning sounds of bird calls and fluttering
wings.
The haze of heat gathers across the far field,
calling summer insects to amass in swarms
before my eyes.
Glasses full of ice clink inside summer juices
squeezed into thirst-quenching relief.
Guests arrive, and the balcony that looks across
the valley below,
fills with a human chorus.
Music springs from the internal piano, as men
with dark skins,
find their way together with cords and
harmonies.
Melding into the spontaneous gyration
of loose hips and laughing lips.
Women fan themselves; men flirt outrageously.
Embarrassing moments pass in silence.

Bowls full of summer fruits, the latest clothes,
grasping hands, pergola lovers entwine.
You, with red curls and Irish skin, reach for me,
pulling me forward into your grasp.
We pretend to dance, your hand stroking my
back.
The warmth creeps up my neck, into my cheeks,
I push you away, feigning heat.
The light fades into evening,
smells of banquet drift along the balcony
calling people into the coolness of the interior
where ceiling fans beat with the rhythm of the
music
and the last of the sun's rays fade into the night.
Your eyes meet mine in silent agreement,
our fingers entwine.
Lead crystal glasses filled with red wine,
carried by white-jacket waiters
are set before the guests.
Courses appear and disappear,
and conversation dances around the room.
I feel the soft fabric of your trousers
brush against my leg, and my skin tingles in
anticipation.
As if reading my mind, you move your body
closer,
and mine responds, falling into the mindset of
love
and a newly married kiss.

A Friend

Geoff Gibbson

Moonlight softly caressed her cheeks
Her eyes sparkled
Oh, how beautiful
Gorgeous.
Do I alone see this?
Why, why do not others
want to carry her away
and stay with her forever
to enjoy the music of her voice
and smile at her jokes,
to be entranced by her enthusiasm for life,
and to savour the subtleness of her perfume.

The gentle touch of her fingers,
the expectation in her eyes
as our lips barely touch.
Oh, what bliss
to feel her beside me.
Our lips meet -
exquisite
what joy.

It is as if there is nothing else in the universe
only the two of us,
together.
A gasp.
Why is my breathing so fast?...
Her head on my shoulder
as we hold each other.
Softly whispered, almost to herself
words of love, of kisses, of peace.

A sliver from a misty memory.
Alone.

The Pressure
of a Name

Sandra Joy

Unborn child: a four-month fetus

"What about Tony?"

"No, all the Tony's I know are womanisers."

"Robert?"

"No, they're always short. I do like the name Chad. But nah, they're all junkies."

Deciding on the first name for a child was a big responsibility, especially when it was going to be an only child. I didn't have the luxury of selecting a few favourite names and dividing them over a family of kids. This baby was going to be my only child, and so his or her name had to be perfect.

"Okay, what if it's a girl. Do you still like Alexandra?"

"Hmm, I always wished that was my name. That's why I considered it. But not anymore; that would just be weird."

"Jessica? That's a pretty name that hasn't been used for a while."

"Yeah, so she would get teased for it being different."

"Kelly?"

"Just the opposite, it's a popular name so she would be normal, average."

Mum and I had been doing this every week since I learned I was pregnant. Every week the same thing. We would go through a myriad of options and finally settle on a name. Then, without fail, I would meet someone with that name and decide I didn't want to put my child through that fate. I think I believed we were all clones, with personalities destined by our first name. Sure, there were articles that support the notion of people living up to their name, but there are more types of people than there are names. It's not scientifically possible for every person with the same name to be identical.

But what if my child inherited that distinguishing feature – the one I associated with their name. I could never forgive myself for coercing their life like that.

Unborn child: a six-month fetus

I had started a journal of names and the reasons I didn't like them. Writing a book of baby names would have been quicker. Why didn't I think of baby name books then? Derr, I could have just bought a book of baby names and crossed-out the definite dislikes, written in the margins any reasons against that name, and colour coded those with potential. Oh, that would have been so much easier.

At the end of my second trimester, my journal had reasons against 48 boys names and 67 girls names. That's it. My child is going to have only one name. A surname.

Surname! What surname do I give them? I had only been thinking about Christian names; I hadn't considered that there were options for the last name too.

Now I had to find five names: a first and middle name for each gender and a last name. Two sequences of names that sound good together, as well as on their own. Two sets of names that suit a baby, toddler, teenager, adult and old person. Five names that don't have any negative associations.

This was impossible. Why, oh why, did I ever allow him to impregnate me.

How do other women do this?

Unborn child: an eight-month fetus

Eight months passed and the weekly impasse continued. I had decided on some of my obligation. The surname would be mine. I didn't like the other option; it just didn't sound good with any of the names that made it to the short list.

I decided on a girl's name at last – Jacinta Kay.

The boy's name had a short list of three: Alex, Chad and Trey. Middle name TBC.

One Friday afternoon, I attended my regular doctor's appointment. Mothers know the ones: where you feel like your body isn't your own, you should just bring a bed into the doctor's office because you spend so much time there, and this person spends more time with your body then your baby daddy.

He asked, "How long have your ankles been swollen?"

Looking down (as if I expected them to change), "I don't know, a week or so. Isn't that part of pregnancy?"

"Not normal pregnancies. Bedrest for you. They need to be elevated. If they haven't returned to normal by Monday morning, I will see you at the hospital."

I obediently spent the weekend in bed but to no avail. One phone call to the doctor's office on Monday morning resulted in me being transported to Singleton Hospital.

Checked and probed, shaved and jabbed, I was informed I was having my baby. "Today. By caesarean."

I had toxaemia and the baby was breach. It was time for this little bundle to join the outside world – and receive a name!

"Nurse, what's the process for registering a baby's name?"

She explained that, after the birth, the hospital issues new mums with the forms. One of them is to be filled out and taken to the local court house where they register the name with Births, Deaths and Marriages. "You have seven days to lodge it."

Phew. I had heard stories of other people not naming their baby straight away.

Decision made.

I am going to wait to see what my baby looks like, and then I will know what name suits them.

The staff were lovely, and counting backwards from ten was as impossible as it was designed to be.

After my operation, I woke slowly in the maternity ward and was given sips of water to help the dry mouth and throat. As my eyes fully opened and my brain realised where I was, I mumbled the words, "Can I see my baby?"

"Of course, I'll go and get him. You had a boy."

A boy. Aww, he can carry on the family name like the old tradition; along with whatever Christian name he looks like.

The nurse pushed a cot, followed by family that quickly surrounded the bed. It was my sister who spoke first, as the nurse handed me my unnamed bundle of joy.

"Meet Robert. He's beautiful."

"Robert? Who named him?"

"You did." The nurse explained. "When you came out of surgery, you announced, 'His name is Robert'. So, that's what's on his name card and bracelet, and that's what we've been calling him."

I didn't have the heart to change it, but first, "How tall is he?"

"He's 52cm. Four weeks early, he's going to be tall!"

Foiled

Bronwyn MacRitchie

It was Sunday morning. My watch read two am. I hastily exited the noisy night club needing to restore balance in my ear drums from the cranked sub woofers and noisy conversation. For twenty minutes, I'd inhaled second hand smoke while my retinas endured assault from strobe lighting and fog lights. I breathed deeply, welcoming the fresh air. This time I was certain she'd spotted me.

I crossed the street to the park opposite not wishing to linger, as raucous couples spilled onto the footpath eager to continue partying elsewhere. I scanned the street searching for the car, but it wasn't there so I strode diagonally through the park. A stray dog circled the rubbish bin, sniffing. The cat perched on the rim, delivered a territorial hiss.

For six months John and I had lived together. His ex-wife, Clare, had decided to take a vacation from her three children, aged five years and under. Months had passed without contact. No letters, no cards, and no phone calls. When I met John, he'd been granted full custody due to Clare's lengthy absence. After nine months, she'd returned, and on advice from legal aid, applied for custody.

Over the months, the children's love for their mother had waned. With her return, the affection, trust and security we'd worked so hard to establish and maintain, could be eroded with the knock of a gavel. We were not married, so legally I had no voice, despite my commitment and love for the children and their father.

At the hearing, the judge awarded full custody to the mother. The children were to be handed over to her immediately. Visitation by the father was at her discretion. Considering the circumstances, it was an astonishing decision.

Since her return, there'd been no visits by her to see the children, and no phone calls enquiring how they were. Both John and I were flabbergasted. We were confident her history would work in our favour.

When Clare came to collect the children, it was the only time we met. It was also the only time I wanted to seriously injure another woman. I kept my emotions flat as I handed over their packed cases. The children were confused. Where are we going? Is Daddy coming?

"Where are you taking them?" John had asked.

"I'll let you know," she'd said.

But she hadn't.

Two days later John received a phone call. From a women's hostel.

I listened against the earpiece to hear what was being said.

"Mr Blake, your son is extremely distressed, and we have been unable to reach his mother for two days. He is not eating and we are rather concerned."

"Two days? They've been there for two days, and she is not with them?"

"You understand we cannot tell you where we are, but we sympathise with your situation."

"I'll come and get them," said John. "Tell me where you are."

"You can speak to your son, Mr Blake, but I cannot tell you where we are. The court will not allow it."

Crackling and muffled voices followed, then a thin, quivering voice spoke.

"Daddy, where's Mummy?"

"Daren, how are you mate?"

"I don't like it here. I don't know anybody. Mummy took us here, then left."

John clenched his hand into a tight fist and punched the sofa.

"Don't worry son."

"Daddy, I want to come home."

"I want that too. How are the girls?"

"They're asleep. Daddy, can we come home?"

After a few feeble promises, John hung up.

"How could she do this?" He paced the room. "How did this happen?"

I knew the question was rhetorical and my reassurances were of no comfort.

By the end of the afternoon and numerous phone calls, legal channels had been exhausted.

John was frantic.

"We will have to do this ourselves," he said. "I know her. She'll be out boozing while the kids are terrified and wondering what's happening."

"And what are WE going to do?" I asked.

"Find out where she is and follow her. Record her movements."

"Record her movements?"

"You can bet she'll think this is a breeze. She's won. Kids are safe. It's Friday night. Party with the boyfriends."

"John. I'm not sure about this." Relationships shouldn't be this complicated.

"She doesn't really know what you look like. Just a brief glimpse when she picked up the kids."

He started pacing again. Arms conducting a clandestine operation.

"John. It's not right."

I had nothing to say so I let him ramble. This was a bad idea.

"All we need to do, is write down where she goes. Easy. Then we have evidence for that poxy idiot of a judge. You go in, sight her, then get out."

"Jeez, John, I'm not cut out for this."

"Change your hair a bit. Wear different clothes. Women change their appearance all the time."

"No."

"I need you," he'd said. "One night, that's all."

That alone should have been a warning. What would I do if it was my child?

"Contact the police. That's their job."

"They won't do anything. I tried."

Regardless, I'd relented. One night had turned into a weekend. We borrowed a car from a friend and had driven around streets to every known drinking hangout in Perth. Some were innocuous buildings where basements concealed the throbbing activity within. I'd been in and out of all of them without seeing Clare. It was like being on a ghastly city tour.

I'm doing this for the children, I kept reminding myself. Finally, with my tolerance for the exercise diminishing rapidly, we spot Clare leaving a club with a group of others.

"Off you go," said John. "Follow her."

"You've got to be kidding," I said. "No chance. I'll do the club thing, but I'm not following anyone on the street."

"We could lose her."

"Where's the next club?"

"Around the corner."

We looped back and forth throughout the city as I tracked Clare and her exuberant entourage. Periodically, a couple would leave the group, until there were six people remaining. Her desire to visit every club had left me exhausted. I wanted to grab the woman and give her a good shake. *Go be with your children. Pretend you actually care about them. Stop partying, you stupid woman.* But that was not up to me. Research for a crime novel would have been a lot more fun than sneaking in and out of pubs and night clubs like a sleezy character in a Raymond Chandler novel.

An unexpected confrontation in one club had left me shaken.

"Don't I know you?" a guy had asked as I stood close to the bar momentarily distracted by the music. It didn't sound like a pickup line, more of an accusation. He looked about eighteen and appeared to still be working out a shaving method. His speech indicated he had exceeded his alcohol limit. I may have been in my late twenties, and not exactly pickup material, but a lone woman in a night club was conspicuous. Behind him, I spotted John's ex weaving her way towards us, a quizzical look on her face.

"Bloody hell," I said, left the bewildered guy, scooted up the steps and ran for two blocks with John in the car following, I was so shaken by the moment.

"Get in the bloody car," he shouted.

"I'm done," I told him slumping down in the seat. "That's it. I can't do this detective stuff anymore. I've got five dollars left. All these cover charges are depleting my finances. This is crazy. She's never going home! She doesn't give a damn about the kids."

"Just one more," he said. "We'll go home then."

"Oh great. Just great."

I paused on the corner at a row of shops. Cobwebs laced across the dust covered items inside. The entire block showed signs of neglect and disuse. Newspapers and unopened letters in the doorways were of more use to the homeless.

I was angry, frustrated and drained. I wanted to go home, have a feed and lie down. My feet hurt because I'd worn low heels instead of flats and my last snack was a packet of lifesavers at eleven o'clock.

Where the hell was John?

This area had a sinister feel about it. It seemed only a few minutes since the disorderly patrons had dispersed from the club. The lights had been switched off and the area was deserted. He should be here, waiting for me.

When a shadow stepped out from a doorway ahead, it startled me. The knife in his hand signalled a shakedown.

"Your bag," he gestured, jabbing the knife in my direction.

"Really?" I peered at the youth dancing from one leg to the other to music I couldn't hear. Knees poked through the frayed jeans and from the acne and sprouting whiskers, I judged his age as late teens.

"Give. Me. Your. Bag." He switched the knife to his other hand and poked it at me.

"Piss off," I said. "Go bother someone else."

He twisted his cap so it sat backwards on his head, then stepped back and forth in a patterned square.

"What are you doing?" John said from the other side of the street. "Give him your bag."

"Where the hell have you been?" I hadn't heard him arrive.

"Give him your bag," John repeated.

The youth had added more steps to his jerky dance. He looked like a drunk prize fighter. When he added a couple of gun twirls with the knife it became absurd. This idiot was preventing me from going home. He turned his cap back around again. An anxious gesture. I wondered if he was a drug addict or an opportunist.

"Lady, if you don't give me your bag *now*, I'll stick you with this knife."

"You've got to be kidding." I stepped towards him, and his dancing came to an abrupt stop.

Two doors behind the youth, another stepped out. He anchored himself in a wide stance, crossed his arms over his chest and glared with as much menace as a disgruntled ten-year-old.

"Oh, wonderful," I muttered. "Backup."

"Jesus woman," said John. "Give him your bag."

"Shut up, John!"

A few streets away, a car revved, tyres squealed then thundered off. The two antagonists exchanged a cursory glance.

I pinched the bridge of my nose in frustration and sighed. I was annoyed, irritated and fed up and had neither the desire or inclination to obey his demand.

"You want my bag?" I removed it from my arm.

"You want my bag?" I repeated, and with rising anger, stepped closer.

"What the hell are you doing?" John said.

Both youths jumped back.

"Right," I said.

I opened my bag, took out my handkerchief, wiped my nose, then upended the entire contents of the bag onto the pavement.

They clanged against the concrete with surprising volume. I threw the empty bag at the youths. It plopped at their feet. They stared, eyes switching from the bag and me, and the items strewn at my feet. Lifesaver wrappers and old shopping lists fluttered amongst my comb, eyedrops, pens, pencils, hand cream and coin purse. The few remaining coins scattered in opposite directions as the lipstick rolled unhurriedly into the gutter.

"There. Have my bag." I remained standing, defiant. Hands on hips. "I'm not in the mood to be robbed tonight."

"Lady you are crazy!" uttered the knife-wielding youth as they both turned and ran.

"Get in the car," said John as I picked up my bits and pieces from the pavement.

"What the hell were you thinking?" he said, as he fastened the seat belt and turned the ignition.

"Never, ever ask me to do anything like that again," I said, glaring at him. "Now drive. Do not speak. Just drive."

Shoes in hand, I staggered through the front door of our house at 4am and stared at the blinking light on the answering machine.

"Someone's left a message," I said, hitting the 'playback' button.

"Mr Blake, this is Andrew, Judge Foster's clerk. Apologies for the late call, but certain details have come to our attention regarding the custody agreement with your wife. Please attend a special hearing in Judge Foster's Chambers at 9am Monday morning. I think you will find it a favourable outcome this time."

The message clicked off announcing the time tag: 10:50 pm, Saturday.

Date Gone Wrong

John Franks

In the vernacular, the phrase, 'getting caught with your pants down', generally refers to any situation in which one gets caught out in a state of un-preparedness. If you are scandalised by the following story, which takes on a more literal tone, I apologise. Read no further.

Like most of my embarrassing moments, I can now see more of the funny side than was apparent at the time. In the early 1970s, I had been 'going steady' with a girl who I fancied something rotten, as some might have said in those days.

Our relationship began and developed as a result of me being asked to be her partner for her making her debut. Making one's entry into society via such a formal process was going out of fashion but, youthful hormones i.e. lust, never goes out of fashion in my experience.

The routine was that on a series of Sunday nights prior to the event, we were required to attend rehearsals for the occasion, and we had fallen into the habit of finding 'parking' spots where we could engage in deep and meaningful conversation, exploring each other's mind as well as some of each other's physical attractions, if you know what I mean. This behaviour did not progress to the final denouement. Mind you, we got close.

On the occasion in question, we had driven to a nearby light industrial area late on a Sunday night. We were the only vehicle in the area. Our conversations mostly began with deep and meaningful topics, or so we thought of them at the time. We were really trying to act like grownups but without the experience of grownups. We were in fact, disguising our feelings by trying to sound like adults, when in reality, we were typically immature twenty-ish young things and, so I thought, falling in love.

Now, you may not be surprised to learn that before long we ran out of words and actions of a rather intimate variety began. In those days, I had a car with a bench front seat, which lent itself to up-close-and-personal activity much more than the single bucket seats of today. Mind you, the steering wheel often cramped our style. On this occasion we decided to climb into the back seat to give greater expression to our actions.

We were well advanced in our social and physical interaction when a car with flashing blue lights swung around the corner and headed straight for us. Our first reaction was to hide, so we ducked down below the window line, out of sight. This was a mistake because it made the car look unoccupied. In that area, what looked like an abandoned car was cause for the police to stop and investigate. They pulled up alongside us and got out with their torches flashing into the car. What they saw was the two of us in the back huddled together on the floor, wearing well, not much. The police must have thought they had won the lottery.

While we were scrabbling for our clothes, they knocked on the window and told us to open it, which we did. They then proceeded to spin us a yarn, which we mostly believed at the time, that some burglary or break-in had occurred nearby, and they were investigating anything suspicious. I must admit we probably looked as guilty as sin but not for the incident they claimed to be investigating. No doubt they were getting an eyeful, Marnie mentioned in her most emphatic and indignant tone, which I later came to realise was one equivalent to that of an air-raid warning, "This is my fiance!". With a straight face and without blinking an eye (which, in the darkness I wouldn't have noticed anyway) they pointed out that it was nothing to do with their 'investigation'.

Still scrambling to make ourselves look decent, theyThe padvised us that it was not safe to be in such an isolated place where criminal behaviour might take place, and they told us to go straight home and stood back from the car. They watched as we got out from the back seat and into the front, after which we slowly, and law-abidingly, drove away.

The drive home was characterised by acute embarrassment. We hardly knew what to say to each other. But, before long, we supposed that they were probably doing their rounds for the same sort of 'investigation' they did every slow night when there wasn't much else happening in the patrol area.

Although I don't know how red Marnie face was, I felt mine must have been about to fluoresce to a point I wouldn't need the headlights on. However, with the optimism of youth, by the time we got home, I think the residual over-riding emotion was one of indignation caused by the realisation that the whole experience was a police prank. However, that didn't detract from the fact that it remains an excruciatingly embarrassing moment never revealed, until now.

Inspired

Oops!

Geoff Gibbson

Have you ever done something, or organised an outing, and afterwards thought, *Well, that didn't go too well, did it?* or, *I could have done a bit better that time?*

I can imagine that many of us have had some thoughts like that. Perhaps not everybody, but I admit there have been quite a few (well, rather more than that) times for myself.

There was the time when the ferry for the work's Christmas party was leaving the wharf. I had stood, looking forlorn as the water swirled away from the propellers. A thought, for some unfathomable reason, came to mind.

For those without white or grey hair, you may not be aware of it, but on TV a long time ago, there was a show called Get Smart about a very incompetent spy who was always saved by his delightfully attractive female assistant. He often said, 'Missed by *thaaat* much', while holding up a hand showing about an inch gap between a thumb and forefinger.

Well, we did not miss the ferry by an inch.

It was much more like twenty feet. It seemed so close and yet, at the same time, so far away.

My wife withdrew her hand from mine. I think she may have been displeased with me. I suppose she had a valid reason to be a little tetchy. It was *her* work's Christmas party on board that vessel.

With hindsight – always a very important ingredient – it would have been a good idea to have left more time to drive into the city to catch the ferry. It was a long trip from home to the wharf near the Opera House steps. However, it did have one lovely outcome: we went into the Opera House and were able to listen to Handel's *Messiah*. Oh, such beautiful music, sung with so much passion.

There was another time when my organisational skills or, more correctly, my lack of them, could have changed the direction my life took.

As a youth, (well, a somewhat sheltered bushie in my twenties anyway) I had at last summoned up enough courage to ask a young lass to go out with me. But, where to? That was the important question. Where could I suggest we go on our first outing together?

It was time to ask some friends. One suggested a restaurant, Colonards, in one of the arcades in Sydney. It was classy yet not too extravagant, quiet and, importantly, there was an entertainer: a tenor sang after the conclusion of the main course. I liked that idea. If I ran out of conversation, or became a bit too self-conscious, we could just listen for a while.

I had made the reservations. Here we were, one table for two, closest to the small slightly raised stage area. Flowers adorned the centre of each table and the white tablecloths were immaculate with their settings of multitudes of knives and forks. The whole restaurant had a feel of restrained elegance. My date looked gorgeous in her white blouse and mid-thigh length green tartan skirt, her long brown hair lying halfway down her back. I was dressed in off-white flairs with a patterned maroon shirt, so typical for the 1970s.

We selected our meals from the large variety on the menu. I smiled when I noticed that my menu showed the prices but hers did not. That was rather quaint, even for then. After some time, during which we chatted, the food arrived. It was delicious. Then the entertainer appeared at the open door at the back of the stage and walked up quite close to where we were sitting.

I had expected a laddie, but instead a beautifully attired lassie appeared, trailing a long blue feather boa. Well, that was great. I appreciate solo male singers but like solo female ones even more.

However, much to my surprise, and even more to my companion's, she did not begin to sing. Instead, she proceeded to dance and twirl around the stage, all the while taking off articles of clothing. Finally, all she had was the blue boa constrictor - oops, feather boa – wrapped around her, covering all the delicate bits. This was happening about six feet from us. I was a bit stunned.

With an almost uncomprehending gaze, my date looked towards the stage, seemingly unable to believe she had been taken by me to a burlesque show for her first outing. Just then, a waiter brought a cup of tea, or was it coffee, to the table for her. However, it was not what she ordered and she burst into tears.

The entertainer did her last few twirls, unwrapped the blue feather thing and, with her back to us, skipped towards the door at the back of the stage, trailing the feathers behind her. How shall I put this with a little decorum? Well, um, she was completely starkers. The young fellow with his hand on the doorknob looked even more stunned than I was! I thought that people's eyes becoming large, their jaw dropping and their mouth opening wide only happened in cartoons. Yet, that is how he looked as the entertainer gaily danced towards him. By this time, my companion was quietly weeping, so it seemed an appropriate time to leave.

Outside, I did my best to convince her that I really had no idea that that particular entertainer would be performing. I really had expected the tenor to sing, as he had done the previous weekend. To this day, I still am not one hundred percent sure she believed me.

One thing I found surprising. She agreed to go out with me again!

As I wended my weary way home to my college cubicle, I reflected on the night and a wry smile came to my face. *Well, that could have gone a bit better. Well, a whole lot better actually!*

That Night

Sandra Joy

There are two-hundred and eleven flowers on the wallpaper opposite my bed. I know, I've counted them many times since that night. *That night*. It seems so long ago, but every time I close my eyes it happens all over again.

Mum taps gently on the door just moments before opening it. She knows I am not getting out of bed to open it. She carries the 'sick in bed' tray as my sister calls it and I can smell the pumpkin soup before I even see the steam. With a shy smile she briefly lowers the tray to show me what's on offer before placing it on the desk beside my bed. Beside the soup is a plate with bread cut into thin strips she calls 'soldiers', a bowl with apple pie and custard, and a glass of orange juice.

Dear Mum. Even without knowing the full story, she doesn't seem to tire of this ritual. Mums have instinct. And patience. I am pretty sure she has persisted in bringing me three meals every day since, despite me telling her I don't want to eat. Come to think of it, I am pretty sure I have only eaten two sandwiches and one banana since he left five days and – I glance at the clock – four hours ago. Oh well. Maybe I will try the soup.

Though still not hungry, I must be feeling better. For the first time I realise that I haven't been to school this week. I vaguely remember her telling me days ago that Liz and Jenny had been calling. Have they stopped? Do friends lose interest that quickly too?

My heart pounds through my chest as I get a flashback to the last phone call I made. I rang his house the next afternoon and his mum told me he had transferred to Brisbane. She asked me if I knew why he would suddenly up and leave and I just slammed the phone down and cried. Angry tears. Sad tears. Tears of relief and fury. How dare he!

Is it possible that the radio has been on all day? Maybe Mum turned it on this morning? Maybe she has been turning it on every morning, but I'm only now tuning in to it?

Meatloaf groans out the rock ballad lyrics:

I want you, I need you.

But there ain't no way I'm ever gonna love you.

Now don't be sad, 'cause two out of three ain't bad

I can't imagine a female ever singing those words. In fact, now I wonder what the writer did to make him say it. Did he also rape his girlfriend, take away her virginity and then leave town?

Part 2:

FIRST

On the Job

First News - Worse News

Tony Lang

Home at last. The Reverend Henry Mobbs glanced through the train window and saw the first signs of the approaching town. He stood and pulled his luggage from the rack. What a relief, he thought, to be back from that week-long, annual church conference in Sydney.

Thoughts of his wife Ellen and the cool manse were now uppermost. He felt a glow of anticipation. Tomorrow – first Sunday of Advent! Sermon already prepared. The liturgy would include the lighting of the first Advent candle. A memory interrupted his pleasant reflection. Last year the Advent candle had almost refused to light. He'd talked it over with his church clerk, Jim Kitchen. "This year," he'd told him, "We'll start with a candle we've already had alight."

He stepped from the train and onto the station. Strange – he couldn't see Ellen. Then he noticed a smiling figure walking towards him – Jim Kitchen, the church clerk! Good man, Jim, but inclined to diffidence. Found it hard to spit out a direct sentence but top value anyway.

"How's things, Jim?'" Henry asked as they strode down the platform; "Any worries?"

"No worries I can think of, Henry."

"Good. By the way, where's Ellen? I thought she'd be here to collect me. Is she playing tennis?"

Jim shook his head. "No, she's not playing tennis. She's in hospital."

The minister stopped in his tracks. "What? In hospital? Why?"

"Well, they think it was the shock."

Reverend Henry Mobbs paled.

"What do you mean; shock? What happened?"

"It was probably the shock caused by the fire."

Henry felt like screaming. Getting information out of Jim Kitchen was like getting money from a miser.

"Quick, Jim – just get me home. I'll drive up to the hospital immediately!"

"I'm afraid I'll have to drive you, Henry. Your car was destroyed in the fire."

"I can't believe this! How did my car catch fire?"

"Ah, um, it was in the garage at the time."

"Do you mean the garage is destroyed too? Please – tell me, what happened. How did the garage catch fire?"

"Er, I think the fire spread from the manse."

For the first time in his life Henry Mobbs felt like committing murder.

"*How did the manse catch fire, Jim?*' he yelled; 'Tell me!"

Jim looked uncomfortable. "I took the Advent candle into the church and lit it. My mobile rang. As I was answering it a gust of wind blew the curtains onto the candle and started the fire. I'm afraid the church is gone too."

By this time, they were at Jim's car. Henry slumped into the seat.

"Just get me to the hospital, please Jim," the minister mumbled.

"Certainly, Henry."

As they drove, Jim said, "There's one piece of good news, Henry" and handed him a paper bag.

Henry stared at it dully. "What's this?"

Jim beamed. "As the church was going up, I managed to race back inside and grab the Advent candle."

Source unknown, but I thank whoever first thought of it and all of those who have shared it since.

A police recruit was asked during the exam, "What would you do if you had to arrest your own mother?"

He answered, "Call for backup."

The Eye of the Needle

Pat Fern

Nathan Wallace watched the young couple discussing the comparative merits of Matchbox cars with their small son. The girl rocked a sleeping baby. The tiny face was peaceful, tiny hands curled against an embroidered blanket. Nathan's throat tightened. He turned away from the only thing he could never buy with his vast wealth.

Unnoticed by the busy shoppers, he strode to the door leading to his private car park. Although it was only the beginning of August, everything his enterprising store manager considered remotely suitable for a Father's Day gift, bore a screaming label.

Nathan owned the chain of stores that linked city to city, town to town across Australia. They were a small part of his empire. Why then did he feel that the family in the toy department were richer than he'd ever be?

His chauffeur was still at lunch, he would have a few precious minutes alone. A figure ducked behind his Rolls Royce as he approached and they started to run. Nathan was quicker. He grabbed a small, struggling body. Frightened grey eyes stared defiantly into his.

"What are you doing here?"

"Nothin', I was only lookin'."

"If you've damaged..."

"I never touched yer car."

Nathan saw that the car was undamaged, which was more than could be said for the boy he was holding. His tatty clothes did nothing to conceal the cuts and bruises on his skinny, dirty body.

"What happened to you?"

"I went onto someone else's patch an' they bashed me up."

"How old are you. Don't you have a home?"

"What do you think? Me Mum's boyfriend chucked me out 'cause I was in 'is way. I can look after meself, I'm sixteen."

"More like twelve, I'd say. Here's twenty dollars, get yourself a meal." The boy's eyelids drooped provocatively. He sidled closer to Nathan.

"Where'dja want it, 'ere or at your place?" Nathan recoiled.

"What are you talking about?"

"All the old guys who give me money want somethin' for it. An' all them questions, I thought you was interested." Once more Nathan was looking at a puzzled twelve-year old. "Don't you want – you know?"

"Certainly not, take the money and go." The boy scrambled away leaving Nathan shaking.

Nathan went home, and even after a few days, the incident still haunted him. Sydney was still euphoric after hosting the most successful Olympic

Games ever. The city was still sparkling from the refurbishing it had received for the benefit of tourists and their money.

Under all the glamour, lay the sad lonely disposable children living in squalor on its streets. The contrast struck him as never before in his sheltered, luxurious life. He had to do something. He had to find the lad who he met in the car park. He had failed the boy once, he had to rescue him.

He didn't even know his name.

The Salvation Army officer looked doubtfully at the tall, well-dressed man so out of place in the stinking alley. He could see the garish lights of Kings Cross reflecting on the gleaming limousine with the chauffeur waiting with professional patience.

"Yes, sir, can I help you?"

"Actually, I was wondering if I could help you, Captain."

"Major – Major Ken Barker. What exactly do you mean?"

Nathan hesitantly told the Major about the boy who had touched him so deeply.

"I understand, I don't think you'll ever find him again. There are plenty more where he came from."

He looked at the expensive suit and the watch that would feed his waifs for a year.

"Meet me here tomorrow in old clothes, minus the car, and watch. I'll show you what you would be letting yourself in for."

Ken Barker doubted he would ever see this would be do-gooder again. Christ's words about it being easier for a camel to pass through the eye of a needle than a rich man to enter into the glory of God crossed his mind as he watched the big car draw away.

Ken was startled when a tall figure detached itself from the shadows the following evening.

"Ok, let's go."

"Welcome to the team – Mr?"

"Nathan. Nathan Wallace."

"*The* Nathan Wallace?"

"I guess so. Keep it to yourself though, I don't want publicity."

For some nights Nathan remained aloof. He watched the Salvationists tenderly lifting filthy, broken bodies. He saw comforting arms going around children and adults. The sheer dirt and smells repulsed him. Ken doubted every night that he would ever see the man again, but each night he returned, although Ken could never quite see why. Whenever they found a young boy, he would peer into their face without touching. Ken knew Nathan was looking for the boy in the car park.

The first time Nathan knelt in the dirt to place a gentle arm round the shaking shoulders of a girl huddled in a doorway, he was rewarded with a wary sidelong glance, and then a radiant smile.

"Come on. Let's get you warm and fed."

From that time on his commitment was wholehearted and sincere.

2006 AD

"Nathan, the shareholders won't stand for you giving away those buildings."

Nathan patted his General Manager on the shoulder.

"Calm down, Alan. I'm not exactly giving away the business. Those buildings have been standing empty for years. If anything, they're a drain on us because we have to maintain them. The Sallies and the Sydney City Mission may as well use them as refuges. Any money I give comes from my personal fortune. It has nothing to do with anybody but me. I intend to see those buildings renovated thoroughly to make decent housing."

"What's got into you, Nathan?"

"Something so wonderful, I have no words."

"All right, have it your own way. If we go broke, there'll be nothing to give."

"That won't happen, Alan. We have more money than we need. What use is it if we can't help those who have nothing?"

Alan James shrugged unconvinced. He would watch Nathan very carefully in future. He didn't seem insane. In fact, he glowed with satisfaction. All he could do was obey orders to keep Nathan's philanthropy a secret.

"Hi, I'm Megan Williams." Blue eyes danced beneath blonde curls. Her white uniform jacket enhanced her trim figure. "Ken told me to report to the tall, skinny guy."

"That sounds like me. Good to have you with us. I'm Nathan Wallace."

He was relieved to see his name meant as little to her as it did to the officers and volunteers who worked with him. Only Ken knew that the richest man in Australia knelt in the filth of Sydney's back alleys, regardless of his navy-blue uniform, and took the homeless into his arms.

The press would have a field day with the great Nathan Wallace 'getting religion' and joining the Salvation Army.

Nathan took care they never found out how he spent his nights. The children were his special interest. He yearned to give them a home and education. He rejoiced when a youngster returned to a good home as a result of his intervention. Other children were placed in homes he built in the country.

Ken Barker was well content. He put a companionable arm round his friend's shoulders as they left for their homes after a particularly harrowing night.

"You did well, Nathan. I'm pleased you made it through the eye of the needle."

"Are you inferring I'm a camel?" Laughing, the two men climbed into their van and drove home.

2007AD

"Wake up, Mr Wallace."

The laughing voice of his secretary broke into his involuntary sleep. His neck ached from resting on his desk.

"Had a heavy night on the town?"

"You could say that, Jeannie. Get me a coffee to keep me awake for the board meeting."

"Give it a miss, sir. We are making record profits so nobody is going to yell at you."

"Maybe I will, tell them I have a date with my office sofa."

"I'll think of something, but you'll have to do something about your hectic social life."

That night Nathan asked Megan to marry him. She accepted joyfully.

"There is something you must know about me before we go any further." Nervously he took her to his office and showed her the extent of his fortune.

"Nathan Wallace, you could have told me that you owned half of Australia sooner."

"I wanted to surprise you."

"So, you are the mysterious person who has given so much so that the homeless have hope and a future. Why didn't you say who you are?"

"I knew that it would put a barrier between me and the others. Ken knows."

"Thank you, Nathan."

"Not me, darling, you know who to thank."

"I thank Him with all my heart for you and the way he has used you."

2009 AD

"I can't believe it, Megan. Where are you?"

Nathan waved the letter as he catapulted through the lounge door. "I've been named Father of the Year."

The identity of the benefactor who had made such a difference to Sydney's dispossessed had leaked, as the media were fascinated with the society wedding of the year. Nathan Wallace marrying an obscure little Salvation Army girl caused a furore in women's magazines, the press, and television. It was inevitable that they would put two and two together and come up with the correct answer.

Megan, who was six months pregnant, eagerly reached for the letter.

"Father to all homeless children. Tireless worker for the destitute."

"The honour should go to Ken, you and all the others, not just me."

"And the glory goes to God." His wife kissed him. "Accept it on behalf of everybody who works for the homeless."

Never a day went by that he didn't think about and pray for the grey-eyed lad in the car park. A shadow crossed his face. Megan knew what he was thinking.

"Sweetheart, you will have to accept that you will never know what happened to him. All you can do is commit him to God and trust Him to care for him."

Nathan held Megan close.

"I'm truly blessed. No one has ever been given so much for doing so little."

The Strawberry Patch

Patricia Ruell

I tumbled out of bed in the dark, nervous because it was my first job. Waving goodbye to Dad in his old EK Holden, I was wide-eyed on the ferry, watching the city waking up, the horizon lit by the sun rising on the new day.

Sue met the ferry on the Stockton side. Almost six feet tall with short hair, she was solidly built. Three other girls joined us and we introduced ourselves. Jo, who had also been on the ferry, was a university student; Wendy and Linda were at school like me.

We all squeezed into the small white car and sped along the road to the song 'I Can't Wait for September'. Sue was telling us in her slow drawl how it was difficult to get female workers. Men caused too much trouble with a female boss.

The two pickers were busy already. Sue introduced Gail, a deeply tanned woman who was also in charge. Our first task was to pull off the old leaves, being careful not to damage the strawberry plants. It was December and the sun beat down strongly. I was glad for the hat that Mum made me bring along. The flies buzzed around incessantly, disregarding the insect repellant we kept on applying.

Linda returned from the little shed in the middle of the field complaining. The country-style toilet had a pan that smelled awful in the summer heat.

By smoko time I felt I had done a good day's work already. I drank some weak tea with lots of milk and sugar and ate a slice of date and nut roll from home. Sue was swearing at Gail in what appeared to be her usual cheery fashion. Gail took out a packet of Bex and tipped one of the powders on her tongue, washing it down with a gulp of tea. The other picker, a middle-aged woman called Mel, told us how many berries she had picked that morning.

Sue warned us, "I've been spraying on the far side of the patch so don't eat any of those berries."

We hadn't realised that we were allowed to eat any berries. After smoko the four weeders went out and gorged ourselves, but the novelty soon wore off. We were carting sawdust now, spreading it neatly down the aisles between the plants.

At knock-off time, Sue drove us back to the ferry. She told us, her conversation punctuated with oaths, that she and Gail used to work in a tomato sauce factory.

It was only three-thirty when I reached the wharf in Newcastle. I decided to visit a school friend who had a job as a shop assistant in a department store.

As I walked along, I thought about the money I would get at the end of the week. My brother always brought home a bulging pay packet from his job at the BHP. He had teased me about my lack of money one day at breakfast. In a huff, I sat reading the jobs section of the newspaper, and saw the job at the strawberry farm.

"You'll never last a day, Patricia," he scoffed, and Mum had looked a little dubious as well.

At the store, my friend was dressed smartly in a black skirt and blue blouse. I had forgotten I was wearing an old straw hat, muddy jeans and a faded t-shirt. It looked like a much easier job at the store. I suddenly looked forward to the time later in the holidays when we would both be dressed in our swimmers, lying on Bar Beach. I left quickly to catch the bus home.

The third day was the worst. I felt stiff and my back ached when I bent over to trim the plants. There was a sudden shower and we put on our raincoats. Sue was cursing as she lugged the pan out of the toilet to empty it on the other side of the property.

Smoko time and the place lit up; even Wendy took out a packet. At the end of smoko, Sue came back into the shed that served as the tea room at one end, the packing room at the other, and said, "You lazy birds had better get a bloody move on!"

The next day I still felt sleepy when I started down the third row with more sawdust, and at first, I didn't notice the new pickers. About twenty years old, their long legs tanned a coppery brown, they seemed to be moving along the rows slowly compared to Mel, and I wondered how long they would last.

Jo, the university student, joined me outside the tearoom where I was eating my lunch in the shade. She usually talked about her boyfriend, or what presents her family had bought for Christmas, but today she wanted to gossip about the new pickers.

"They keep talking about the party they went to on Saturday night," she said.

"They won't last long," I observed.

I was right about them being slow. They had another chance the next day, but the day after, Sue gave them the sack.

Friday was another hot day. At the morning break we sat drinking our cup of tea while Sue glanced at the paper.

"Here's an article you'd like, Mel," she said to the other picker, a thin woman who looked as though she had been bleached by the sun. Sue put the paper in front of her. "What do you think about that, eh?"

Mel looked awkward. Gail came into the room and walked over to her usual chair, Bex packet in hand. It took her a few minutes to work out what Sue was up to.

"Leave the girl alone!" Gail exclaimed at last.

"I can't read," the picker explained to us, adding with a wry turn to her lips, "Do you think I'd be stuck here if I could do something else?"

Mel took her top off after smoko, working in just her shorts and bra. It was okay, because we were all women, weren't we? So, the rest of us did the same. By lunchtime, we were hot and thirsty, so we put our tops on again and walked down to the service station not far down the road to buy some cold cans of coke. There was a helicopter flying overhead, and an ambulance and a police car flashed past. At the service station, the attendant told us there had been a bad accident on the road, and we shivered in the heat. The sky was too blue and the sun too bright for tragedy.

Sue told us at lunchtime that once we finished with the sawdust, we could pick up our pay and go. The good news was that there was another week's work if we wanted it. By three we were finished and had a cup of tea while she gave us our money. It was a bit like speech day at school. Jo came in first with twenty dollars, then Linda and Wendy with eighteen dollars. Finally, I opened my envelope to find fourteen dollars. The going rate was thirteen, Sue told me, but she gave me a dollar bonus.

"And youse all done a bloody good job!" she said.

The wage packet was based on age, and I was the youngest. It wasn't much, but it was the first pay packet I had ever earned.

When I arrived home, I saw my brother had finished work as well.

"So, did you get your pay packet, sis?" he asked, sitting on one of the chrome kitchen chairs.

"Yes," I replied.

"So, how much did you get?" he asked.

I avoided the question and went off to shower and change out of my dirty clothes. When I came back, he had gone through my bag.

"Fourteen dollars!" he exclaimed. "Are you sure they didn't rip you off?"

I was annoyed. "No. She gave me a dollar extra."

"I guess you told them you weren't going back for that sort of money."

Fourteen dollars was better than nothing.

"No, I'm going back next week. There's still more weeding to do."

He went off to ring his girlfriend leaving me fuming. Later, after dinner, I had another look at the pay envelope. I now had twenty dollars! My brother must have slipped in some more notes. Grateful for the extra money, I started planning how I was going to spend it.

The Red Coat

Judy Turner

In January 1958, aged fourteen years and ten months, I began my first full-time job as a clerk-typist in a Sydney city office. A month earlier, my father had told me he couldn't afford to keep me at school for another two years, thus ending my dream of doing the Leaving Certificate and going to teachers' college.

My parents struggled to maintain our family of six plus Grandma on Dad's single wage, and I knew the small amount I would contribute was important.

When I brought home my first pay packet, Mum helped me work out a budget. My mother was a budgeting whizz. How she fed and clothed us with the meagre sum of money she had each week is still a mystery to me.

She told me the amount expected as my weekly board. Then we worked out a list of my expenses: a weekly train ticket to and from work, entertainment, a visit to the movies and maybe a ticket to a dance. But most important of all was my clothing budget.

My wardrobe at the time comprised: my redundant school uniform and lace-up school shoes, three old everyday dresses and one 'best' dress, sandshoes and my leather flat shoes. For Christmas, she and Dad had bought me a pair of high heel shoes and a white cardigan, and before I started work, Mum asked a cousin to make me two cotton summer skirts and blouses. So, with this basis for my summer wardrobe, we planned for the months ahead.

We shopped the next day. I purchased three pairs of nylon stockings (unused to the fragility of nylons, I had already laddered two pairs of stockings that week). Then we found a very smart navy and white spotted dress and put it on layby.

"When you pay off the dress, you should plan your winter wardrobe," said Mum. "A woollen twin-set and straight skirt would be a good start, but, most important of all, you will need a warm coat."

The red coat in the window of a local shop caught my eye about six weeks later. I went in and looked at the price tag. It was very expensive. I tried it on, snuggling into its warmth, pulling the collar up around my neck, rubbing my cheek against the soft wool and pushing my hands into the deep, silk-lined pockets. Then I took it off and hung it back on the rack.

"Put it on layby," said Mum when I told her. "It's important to have a warm coat to get to and from work. Railway platforms can be freezing in the winter. You should have time to pay it off before it gets too cold. You can borrow my raincoat until then." But, of course, I knew I'd rather freeze than be seen in Mum's navy gabardine raincoat.

We lived in a small two-storey terrace house in Burwood, a western suburb of Sydney. Mum and Dad had the front upstairs bedroom, my two young brothers another, and my eight-year-old sister and I shared the third small bedroom. Grandma slept downstairs in what was originally the front parlour of the house.

In May of that year, Grandma had a heart attack and died. She had lived with us since my birth. Life without her hobbling down the hall, shaking her walking stick at one of us, or dishing out some piece of advice, seemed unimaginable. Hers was my first funeral, and I found it horrendous. I had nightmares afterwards in which I heard Grandma calling out as the clods of earth thudded onto her coffin.

A week after the funeral, Mum suggested I might like to move into Grandma's room. I shook my head.

"Oh no, Mum," I said. "It will always be her room."

Grandma's bedroom door remained closed, a heartbreaking reminder of her absence.

The following Friday, I fell while dashing up the stairs of Burwood railway station, shattering the heel of one of my shoes, grazing my knee and shredding my stocking. I missed my train and the next one was due in fifteen minutes. There wasn't time to go home for new stockings and my flat shoes. I ducked into the ladies' toilet, took off my stockings, washed my knee, and then stood shivering on the cold, windy platform, awaiting the train and planning my next move.

I limped, lopsided and late, into the office and apologised to my manager, explaining what had happened. She pulled out a first aid kit and a pair of spare stockings from the bottom drawer of her desk.

"Go and fix up that knee. You can replace the stockings later."

She suggested I buy a new pair of shoes at lunchtime, but I knew I didn't have enough money to do that.

Even if it was possible to fix the splintered heel, my shoes wouldn't be ready for work by Monday. Also, I was going to a dance that night and *couldn't possibly* wear my flatties. My pay packet was due late that afternoon. I would have a half-hour between the close of work and when the shops shut.

A new pair of shoes would mean I would be short of Mum's board and would have to make it up the following week. And, of course, I wouldn't be able to pay anything off my layby. I did my sums. No red coat for at least another month.

On a Saturday morning two weeks later, Mum called me into Grandma's room. The transformation was unbelievable. The room smelt of floor polish and lavender instead of Grandma's rose-scented talc. Gone were the wheelchair and invalid paraphernalia, the holy pictures and all grandma's clutter.

"I did it up a bit," Mum said. "I think you deserve your own space now you're working." She had made new lace curtains to cover the blind and she'd dyed Grandma's white crocheted bedspread blue. The room looked so spacious and different.

"Mum, it's lovely. Thank you."

"I have another surprise," she said. "Look in the wardrobe." I opened the wardrobe door. Gone were all Grandma's dresses and hanging there instead was my new red coat.

My Worst Ever Christmas Present

Tony Lang

I t happened while I was a chaplain in the Regular Army.

I was posted to a military base in WA and we'd been there as a family for nearly three years.

About September I received a posting order from WA to Oakey Qld, to take effect immediately because of a situation that had developed there.

That meant Janet would have to stay in WA with the family. I wouldn't be back for the uplift (removal of furniture, family, cats, dogs etc) until nearly Christmas.

This is not unusual in the Defence Force – military personnel posted before families can be uplifted.

Upon arrival at Oakey Aviation Centre, I had to take care of a very sad situation, after which I made a point of finding my way around the base, meeting soldiers, commanding officers, and so on.

There was a strong Military Christian Fellowship (MCF) on the base. They decided to put on a barbie to welcome new personnel posted to Oakey and invited me as the new chaplain.

It was the usual barbie in the backyard of someone's married quarter, as Army homes are called; snags and chops, a few drams and pints and lemonades and things ... heaps of kids running about. I was made very welcome.

About half an hour after the barbie got under way the lady of the house called me over: "Tony – there are two people asking after you – two ladies. They ... um, are a little odd looking, but they said they know you and asked for Major Lang. They're in the lounge room."

Right at that moment the back door burst open – and two of the oddest looking. females I've ever seen ran in! They were robust young women – more bust than ro, you understand, and both blonde. Each a wore skimpy top resembling an army uniform, and each had on a pretend Army General's cap. Everyone just stared, mouths agape.

The two screamed "SURPRISE!! Happy Christmas from Janice, Tony!" and dropped the skimpy tops as they ran to me, bared buxom bosoms bouncing brazenly. I was transfixed. They grabbed me and planted lots of kisses, singing a little Christmas ditty – I can't remember the words but "ditty," "little bitty" and "titty" featured.

I could have died on the spot. I'll never forget the looks of the members of the Military Christian Fellowship ... absolute horror, amazement, shock, disbelief.

The laughing strippers then gave me a big card from my wife – Janice – and suddenly the truth hit – They'd come to the wrong house! The soldiers' wives hurried the two strippers outside.

It turns out that in the very next street there was another new arrival on the base – a Major Tony Lane, a RAEME officer whose wife's name was Janice, not Janet. His wife and family were also back at their former base, waiting for their uplift.

The soldier on the gate had directed the strippers to the wrong party!

They had probably said 'Major Lane' but the soldier heard 'Major Lang'.

Major Tony Lane's wife Janice catered to her hubby's tastes. I don't think Janet would have thought to do that in a thousand years.

It was probably one of the best Christmas presents for Major Tony Lane – but the worst one Major Tony Lang ever had!

Shake up for a Rookie Cop

Maggie Rose Carr

I was on my first solo patrol. The field training officer who was following behind me, monitoring and assessing my movements, had been called to a traffic accident. He told me to finish my rounds and head back with my report.

Before I arrived at the station, a call came in for me to check out an issue in a block of flats nearby. Only just able to catch the address and that backup was being sent, the line crackled and went dead.

Maybe a storm was on the way?

Leaning my head out of the car window, I noticed angry clouds forming in the early evening sky.

Yep, definitely a storm coming.

The previous 12 months of 'mockup' sessions, including lectures, dummies with fake blood, and in field training, made me feel confident that I could pretty much handle any situation now.

The term 'sink or swim', which a lot of the more experienced officers had used during training sessions, echoed in my ear. I was determined to swim.

Turning the car around, I headed for the destination.

Many of the dilapidated buildings in the area had since been demolished and smart new town houses stood in their place. The address I searched for was tucked in behind them, in one of a few forgotten streets still in disrepair. Its inhabitants waiting for relocation.

The block of flats was a dismal sight. Some of the windows were cracked, the glass held together with boards and tape. Rubbish and empty cans littered the pavement. A couple of stray cats wailed at me as I rushed up the broken cement stoop and dashed inside, just in time to miss the first drops of rain.

I surveyed the lurid, uninviting space of the foyer that greeted me.

Next to the entrance was a dilapidated, doorless cupboard that someone had made a vain attempt to repair. Bright blue paint stuck to its outside in uneven brush strokes.

An old office chair with a broken arm rest, torn leather seat and missing castor wheel, offered a precarious resting place for visitors. Faded, peeling wallpaper made its way slowly down the walls towards the bare timber floor.

The building was noisy. Voices shouting. Babies crying. It definitely was not 'the ritz'.

Checking the number of the flat against the list near the stairs, I mused to myself, *just my luck, it had to be the top floor.*

There were four altogether.

I shuddered. It was going to be a long climb.

Faces filled with curiosity, popped out of some of the doors as I hurried past on my way up. I had heard stories of some of the dire goings on in this neighbourhood and I wondered about what might be waiting for me.

Reaching the top level, I paused to catch my breath.

With cautious steps I proceeded along the dark narrow hall. Passing three other flats on the way, I noticed this floor was quiet, eerily quiet. Maybe these flats were vacant?

The enormity of the situation suddenly hit squarely home. I was first there. First to secure the scene. Not knowing what to expect, I swallowed hard and pushed on the half open door of the flat.

The stench of urine and cheap liquor hit and overwhelmed me. I held my breath and entered.

An old man was sitting on the floor cradling a young woman's head in his lap. Blood had congealed on the side of her head from a large gash.

The woman's unblinking eyes peered into the man's face, as if asking – "Why?" Her body lay still, peaceful.

The man's face was uncomprehending distraught. His tears fell lightly onto her forehead and dripped down between the strands of her hair.

"What has happened here?" My voice was almost inaudible, as if I had not said it.

But – It was enough to make him bow his head away from my gaze. He began to sob. Heartbreaking, gut-wrenching sobs. "Help me," he begged, "you have to help me."

Reminding myself of my training, I tried to remain impartial. "Sorry sir, I am unable to do anything for you at the moment. Please stay as you are, so the area can be processed." I asked his name, but he just shrugged and looked away.

Making the decision that I should check if the woman was still alive, I held two fingers to the side of her throat. There was no pulse and I observed that she had stopped breathing.

I asked the man, "how long has she been like this." He looked at a small clock on the wall adjacent to me and murmured, "about half an hour, I think."

As considerable time had passed, I realized that CPR would probably be out of the question. I sighed and tried to be sympathetic.

"It's OK, someone else should be here soon."

I tried to call the station. No signal. *Blasted storm*, I muttered to myself.

Feeling the need to do something, I started to take notes.

The woman looked about 20-25 years old. She was so young, and indeed pretty. Her dress was bloodied and in disarray. I had a sudden impulse to cover her vulnerability. Shifting my attention, I focused on the old man. He was a shell. His faded, worn clothes hung loosely about his emaciated form. His feet were bare and dirty.

The man's sobs had descended into a soft moan. He looked up at me, his eyes red and swollen, left to rot in this God forsaken place. I felt a sense of pity for him, a wasted life, sharing the room with another, fresh and new, snuffed out prematurely.

Heavy rain and wind began to lash at the tiny single window, begging to be allowed in to wash away this abhorrence. I felt trapped, trapped in this nightmare.

Taking a breath, I diverted my angst by concentrating on the state of the flat.

The room was dimly lit with a single globe hanging from the ceiling. A small double bed squashed itself against the wall. It had a coarse blanket hanging from one side. There was not much space left for any other furniture, apart from a small chair, tipped over onto its side; the remains of faded velvet cloth clinging to its seat.

Unmatched, assorted crockery was stacked up on a lopsided bench. A washing bowl was upside down on the floor. Soap splatters covered the bench and dripped down the walls. There were several smashed plates next to the bowl. It was obvious a struggle had taken place.

The wind had subsided slightly, but the room grew cold. It was an icebox. I shivered. The man pulled at the blanket that hung off the side of the bed and attempted to cover the woman. "No," I tried to sound firm, "please sir, you mustn't disturb anything. I'm sure it won't be much longer". He frowned and nodded slightly.

I asked again, "Can you please tell me your name sir?" Still no answer, just a blank stare.

By now I was starting to become a little unhinged. *Remember your training Rookie! Stay calm. Keep focused. Do the job!*

I tried to call the station *again*. Still no signal. Where *was* that *damn* backup?

A knock at the door startled me. *Thank God,* I shuffled my feet and adjusted the collar on my shirt as two constables entered boldly. Their faces were stern, blank.

Small droplets of water jumped from their winter jackets and plopped quietly onto the floor, disappearing between the cracks of the faded lino tiles.

The constables were followed by a stout, gentlemanly figure. A long damp overcoat hung limply across his shoulders, and he carried a small leather satchel with the word 'Sarge' printed in faded gold lettering. He looked assured, confident, and to my astonishment, not bothered too much by the situation. He briefly introduced himself, and promptly started to take his notes. His manner made me feel a little uneasy.

"You can get up now," Sarge said to the man. His voice was harsh, unforgiving.

The man slid himself out carefully from beneath the woman. The action caused her body to move slightly. It shocked me. Holding onto the side of the bed he slowly pulled himself up and hobbled across the room. The light bulb above his head accentuated the deep crevices in his face.

The endless questions Sarge fired at the poor wretched soul, were greeted with long silent pauses.

It was an eternity, but they finally came. A woman from forensics and three ambulance men.

I had managed to keep myself together as the evidence was being collected, photographs taken, and the woman's lifeless body was carried away.

The old man was now a suspect. I hoped that he was innocent as I watched him being taken back to the station. It was only then that I realised for me it was finally over.

My hands started to shake, and I looked at my feet embarrassed.

"It's OK Rookie, you'll get used to it, we've done all we can for now," Sarge encouraged.

He had been given keys to lock up and we placed the 'POLICE LINE DO NOT CROSS' tape across the door.

He breathed a sigh of relief and his manner seemed to soften a bit.

"Ya know Rookie, it does get easier, although you never really get hardened to it, but you have to take control. It's expected. You're the one in charge. It's a bit of a façade really and sometimes even *I* go home and cry, especially when it involves kids."

His words made me relax a little and I realised that he must have been new to this once himself. He smiled and added, "don't worry Rookie, I'll keep an eye on ya. I should have been here first. Bit hard getting thrown in the deep end, eh?"

I nodded and smiled back at him, quietly relieved.

On our way back down the stairs, Sarge told me about a couple of the funny situations he had been in. It made me chuckle and I was beginning to feel even more at ease.

We finally arrived at the bottom and stepped out into the street. The rain had stopped. The night was still. The air calm and fresh. Soft clouds were starting to break away to reveal a few twinkles in the night sky.

My thoughts turned to the old man. What had really happened that night? It wasn't up to me to decide that. I was just low rank. As my eyes followed Sarge making his way back to his car, I wondered, did I have the makings of a good cop?

Yes! I was determined I wasn't going to let him down.

Source unknown, but I thank whoever first thought of it and all of those who have shared it since.

Just a tap on the shoulder:

A passenger in a taxi leaned over to ask the driver a question and gently tapped him on the shoulder to get his attention.

The driver screamed, lost control of the cab, nearly hit a bus, drove up over the kerb and stopped just inches from a large plate glass window.

For a few moments everything was silent in the cab. Then, the still shaking driver said, "Are you OK? I'm so sorry, but you scared the daylights out of me."

The badly shaken passenger apologised to the driver and said he didn't realize that a mere tap on the shoulder would startle the driver so badly.

The driver replied, 'No, no, I'm the one who is sorry – it's entirely my fault. Today is my very first day driving a cab. I've been driving a hearse for the past twenty-five years.

Rosemary's First Outing

Tony Lang

The thin man sat huddled on the floor in a corner of the room. His hands, splayed out, white on the bare board floor, moved nervously. The light below the cheap lampshade cast little more than a yellow glow, the shadows emphasising the drabness and filth of the place.

Standing over the thin man was another man, his dark coat adding to the dark of the room. The thin man looked up, hoping to see a spark of pity. He saw none – only a hard, cold implacable hatred that elevated his fear.

"What do ya want, mate? You knock on me door, I opens it and ya deck me." He tried to sound indignant but failed.

The other spoke. "I've come with a message, Felicio. Do you have any idea who from?"

"You must be from Ryan!" shrilled Felicio. "Look mate, tell Ryan I'll get 'im the money! I'll have it tomorrow – I got another batch I'm makin' up! The money will be there tomorrow!"

The other man shook his head. "I'm not from Ryan, but thanks for the information. No – this message is from a grieving mother. It's about her daughter. A country kid comes to the city for the first time. Meets the wrong crowd. Gets introduced to ice. She dies. You made the ice, Felicio. Remember Rhonda? Her death made the papers."

Felicio felt a new fear. That voice: flat, cold. Emotionless.

"Oh – by the way," the dark-coated man added – "your business partner who met a nasty end last week – how sad!"

Felicio's nervous fear turned to terror. "That – that was you? You killed him? I – I was gunna give up makin' the stuff – I needed money – I owed Ryan – he was gunna kill me if I didn't get it – I didn't know the girl – she was just a client. I'm so sorry! I cried when I read in the paper she died! I dunno who you are anyway. Who are ..."

"Stop babbling! I suppose you see it as just one of those tragedies, Felicio, that can happen to anyone. She was just in the wrong place at the wrong time. Is that the way it was?"

The thin man noted the change of tone with relief. Now the man sounded quite reasonable. *Perhaps,* he thought, *I can talk my way out of this.*

"I never killed no one, Mr ... What did you say your name was?" The big man's cold stare froze the question. "Okay, okay! All I wanted was some extra dosh. I didn't mean that anyone should die. She must have been allergic, or somefink."

"Indeed, she was, so it must have been her fault."

Felicio's face brightened a little. "Well, yeah in a way I suppose it was. I mean, I didn't force her to take ice ..."

"So much for your remorse, Felicio. You killed her." Now the voice was harder, colder.

The thin man was silent.

"Felicio, I've decided to introduce you to a friend of mine. She's a lady, and her name is Rosemary."

Felicio's expression was almost comical. "What?"

"Her name is Rosemary. Would you like to meet her?"

"Ah, sure. Why not? Why do you want me to meet her?"

"She has something to give you."

It dawned on the thin man that he was dealing with a maniac. Better to humour him.

"Where is she, this Rosemary?"

"She's here." The big man put his hand in his coat pocket and produced a pistol. 'I don't think you're going to like what she's about to give you, Felicio," he added.

Felicio stared at the gun and screamed. It was cut short as Rosemary spat death.

The two detectives searched the dead man's room, carefully looking for clues: Detective Inspector Jim Harvey had a florid countenance and a deceptively slow and deliberate manner. Detective Sergeant Laurence Hassan was the opposite: slender, dark-eyed and quick. In one corner of the room a police pathologist was examining Felicio's corpse. The forensics team busily dusted for prints.

At last, the pathologist stood. "Not much to tell," she told the detectives. "Looks like the killer gave this man a bit of a belting before taking him out.

Single shot to the forehead – dead-centre - pardon the pun – just like the other one. I'd say the same killer did this job, using, I suspect, the same nine-millimetre pistol. I'll confirm that later when I get this man onto the table."

The two men sat at a small table in the detectives' offices at the Local Area Command. Occasionally they dipped into a bag of hot chips that sat on the table with their take-away cappuccinos.

Hassan selected a chip, ate it and wiped his fingers on a paper towel. "The pathologist's report indicates that the round she removed from Felicio's skull was from the same weapon used in the first killing. Find it and we've found our killer."

Harvey nodded. "Be nice to wrap it up before I go back."

"I imagine things must be quieter in the Wagga LAC, Jim," Hassan commented. "You've been up here three weeks and you've walked into two murders. You'll be glad to get back to the bush when my boss returns after his leg operation. It's a pleasure having you here on secondment."

Harvey smiled his thanks. "Getting back to the latest murder, I'm inclining more and more to the view that these two killings could be the start of a turf war among the crims. I mean, so far only 'Smiley' Ryan's men have been targeted, and he's the drug king around here. Even the local papers are suggesting a possible drug war. I'd like you to get the troops working on the other two criminal organisations. Let them know we're not joking about this. We won't tolerate a drug war. See if you can find out anything that might suggest someone's trying to muscle in on Ryan. I doubt if there's anything random about these murders."

Hassan nodded. "Will do ... and you?"

"I'll have a look at a couple of other possibilities. First, maybe the murders were the result of a disgruntled client, or non-payment of debt. Even Ryan could have arranged that if they owed him money. I'll look for leads and get back to you if I find anything of interest."

Patrick 'Smiley' Ryan sat at his desk in his plush office. Lights from surrounding high-rises failed to make an impact through the specially tinted windows. No opportunities for possible snipers to see inside. The office lights were on 'dim' mode, which Ryan preferred. The dark room reflected his dark life. Before him was a large pile of ledgers, mainly to do with his corrupt business dealings. A couple of them dealt with his legitimate businesses which his corrupt wealth allowed him to buy. It was an excellent arrangement.

Others who had sat on the other side of his desk, usually quaking with fear, had wondered how he came by the nickname, 'Smiley.' It was hard to imagine he had ever smiled. His eyes were like dark rocks ... hard, cruel, and his mouth had been described as a knife slash on a wheat bag. The only time Ryan smiled was when he had the opportunity to kill someone. He enjoyed it. He didn't have to do that now. He paid others to do it for him and therefore avoid any misunderstandings with the police.

The deaths of Felicio and his cohort bothered him. His spies could find nothing to suggest dirty work, on the part of his criminal rivals. They all lived together in an uneasy peace. No one wanted a war. There's no winner in a war but the police.

Ryan's thoughts drifted to the two heavies he'd brought up from Melbourne to give him extra protection – two very nasty men indeed. Psychopaths. Killed for pleasure. Enjoyed watching their victims die slowly. Ryan offered himself one of his rare appreciative smiles.

He glanced at his Rolex. It was ten minutes to midnight. He'd tidy up, then get escorted home by his two bodyguards.

Suddenly the door opened and a man walked in. At first Ryan thought it was one of his trained killers. He looked up angrily. No one opened his office door without a polite knock.

"Wha – " He got no further. The intruder was in black, even to a dark hat which all but obscured his face. All he could make out were cold, implacable eyes. His hand moved towards his top drawer and the Beretta automatic.

"Don't." The voice was cold, hard. The dimmed office lights shone dully on the pistol pointed at Ryan. He dropped his hand – this time to the hidden switch under his desk. His fingers found it and pressed hard.

The stranger appeared almost amused. "Press all you like. Your thugs won't hear you."

"Who are you?"

"No need to bother you with that. I'm here about the small matter of a dead girl. She died of a drug overdose – the poisonous brew you and your thugs peddle. She was my niece."

Ryan shrugged. "I'm very sorry she died. If you take that gun out of my face I can pay you compensation within reason. Name a price."

"You're the head of giant octopus of evil, Smiley. Cut off the head and the tentacles will wither. The other organisations will rush in for the kill. Chaos will follow. It will be the end of the octopus, Smiley."

Ryan pushed the buzzer under his desk and held it down. He smelt his own growing fear. Where were those two fools?

The big man laughed quietly, briefly. "No need to push that button, Smiley. I introduced your two killers to Rosemary."

Ryan stared at him. "Are you telling me that those two went off with a whore?"

The big man stared back. "You shouldn't have called Rosemary a whore, Smiley. You've insulted her and you've insulted me – that's a real no-no."

He shot Ryan between the eyes.

Downstairs, he stepped casually over the two dead killers, stepped outside and left the door wide open. The police, he thought, would be very interested in the ledgers.

The prediction the big man made to Ryan proved to be correct. The papers screamed drug war. With the damning evidence of the ledgers, Ryan's empire collapsed. The other two criminal organisations blamed each other and fought. The police moved in. Dozens of arrests were made. The surviving drug empires imploded.

The two police officers shook hands on the steps of the LAC.

"That should be enough excitement to last you for a month or two, Jim," Hassan said. "Of course, we'll never find out who did the killings. They'll close ranks there. You know, I wouldn't mind swapping with you for a bit, lead a quieter life for a while. Chase a few sheep and cattle duffers."

Harvey thought of Hassan as his unmarked police car left the M7 and headed off up the Hume highway, towards Wagga Wagga, and he smiled. Hassan was a good man; an excellent detective. He'd enjoy working with him again sometime.

He stopped at Pheasants Nest for fuel and a coffee. He drank the coffee in the car as he reflected on the success achieved in the city. Managing to grab that brief secondment in the city had worked wonders. Three illicit drug syndicates destroyed, and he'd made a good friend in Laurence Hassan.

His thoughts drifted to Rhonda. Her death had been avenged.

He glanced briefly at the hidden compartment under the dash that was Rosemary's home. This was her very first outing as a righter of wrongs. He hoped there would be more. He sensed Rosemary enjoyed doing what she was made to do. She had done a great job in the city. He owed a lot to Rosemary.

First Encounters with the Foreign Legion

George Haith

An opportunity arose to visit Corsica, the Scented Isle in the Mediterranean. However, this wasn't to be a leisurely tour of Napoleon's birthplace as the trip in question was along Grande Randonne 20, one of a network of trails throughout France.

It nominally takes fourteen days to complete and is rated as the most beautiful route in Europe. It is also one of the toughest, given a length of 180 kms with over 10,000 metres of climbing and, frustratingly, descending.

The route runs north-south but the mountain ridges run north east-south west, so its profile looks like a queen stage on the Tour de France. We cheated a little, by using a bus from the airport to reach Col de Bavella, a camp-ground one day's walk up from the southern end of the route. It is set in a pine forest with the added luxury of a water tank. However, from that point onwards, heading north, we would be on or above the tree line at altitudes up to 2,400 metres, trying to avoid sheep and wild pigs as we would be drinking off the land. Suffice to say it was cold at night and while singing in the rain is fun, sleeping in it is a different matter.

Sleeping arrangements consisted of a down-filled sleeping bag, laid on top of a large heavy-gauge PVC bivouac bag which itself lay on a length of low compressibility foam. This combination kept the sleeping bag clean and insulated while providing potential shelter (inside the bivvy bag) in the event of rain.

Getting into the PVC bag while wrapped in the sleeping bag required a degree of dexterity beyond most of us, so I simply slit it down one side and laid on a single layer of plastic, ready to wrap the other half over me if need be. The problem was that condensation inside the bag resulted in us being almost as wet as if we had stayed on top, so when it rained, judging when the pros outweighed the cons was essential for a comfy night.

We got off to a bad start, with some of the group making a fire surrounded by rocks which were used to support a billy can for cooking. Slips, slops and curses later it was obvious we needed to lift our game if we were going to survive like this for two weeks.

We bedded-down for the night, sleeping bags radiating-out from the hub formed by the dying embers of the fire. But not dead enough as during the night, the wind got up and I awoke to the sound of intruders in the camp.

The guy next to me was also awake so we got our torches out, whispered a count-down and spotlighted the two male intruders, who promptly froze in our beams. That was the point when I realised how helpless we were, effectively cocooned in straight-jackets.

Fortunately, the intruders were only concerned about embers blowing off the fire which we promptly doused, thankful we hadn't set fire to ourselves or the surrounding pine forest. No harm done but another lesson learned. Next morning, we made a proper trench fire in best Boy Scout fashion and things started to look up. As it turned out, we only met one other group of walkers on the trip but had several encounters with the locals.

Previous trip reports showed that our next bivouac spot was vulnerable to wild pigs. Setting up my sleeping area, I chose a rock platform over a shallow excavation so I was protected on that side, while I used rocks to build a wall around the rest of the sleeping bag. It was an effective sangar as events later that night were to prove.

We hadn't been asleep long when snuffling from over the wall revealed lots of curious pigs, some with tusks, but fortunately the animals were only the size of a conventional piglet. Even so, lying on the ground, looking up, a set of tusks can be quite intimidating! There were cries for help from some of the other sleeping bags, resulting in much ado for a while, but the pigs then seemed to decide that they had made their point and the rest of the night was uneventful. It highlighted the benign nature of wildlife in the UK (midges not withstanding) compared to the realities of continental Europe where a range of beasts could cause havoc.

The following morning, with a precious few minutes to spare, I indulged in a spot of birdwatching, looking at what seemed to be a bird of prey patrolling the peaks nearby. Amazed at this commitment (it effectively made me the top-weight in a mountain goat handicap) I was asked what I expected to see on the trip. My reply was the hope for a vulture or two, not realising that I was looking at a juvenile Egyptian vulture at the time. Beware of what you wish for!

Our first encounter with Corsicans was next day on the edge of the tree line where we found a timber slab/shingle roof construction like a Tasmanian trapper's hut. This was a one man operation used for cheese making, the back wall lined with a zig-zag of planks supporting hand-sized wicker baskets with cheeses curing in them. Food hygiene inspectors would have got writer's cramp but we weren't fussy, given our diet of dehydrated food, and tucked-in to a delicious soft cheese at one franc a slice, the circular cheese hacked-up with a trusty sheath knife. The milk was from flocks of sheep run in the high summer pastures, cared for by shepherds ranging from teenagers to wizened men of indeterminate age.

At night, we sometimes heard the tinkling bells of an approaching flock and the shepherd would eventually appear and stop for a chat with our leader, Tom. He was just back in Europe from a couple of years of voluntary work in PNG and his French, our schoolboy version and Corsican were effectively three different languages. Even so, we managed to follow the conversation thanks to the World Game and Le Bobby Charlton, Le Denis Law. Apparently the soccer team from the Corsican capital, Bastia, were in the cup final against Dieppe that year.

One section of the route took us through an alpine herb field. Walking in single file, we were effectively a linear mortar and pestle so all of us, but especially those of us at the back, were enveloped in a heady vapour. This wonderful aroma undoubtedly lightened our packs but may also have befuddled the brains up front.

After a while, I saw large signs nailed to the trees on our left with words like, ATTENTION, or ARRETEZ VOUS in red, which suggested there was something awry. A process of Chinese whispers was conveying this to our leader up at the front when we were all brought up short by wild shouting from our left.

The source of this outrage was only clad in boots and shorts, but what really grabbed our attention was on the tree-top high platform next to him; a tripod mounting a short-barrel heavy machine gun. The barrel appeared to be short, for the simple reason it was pointing straight at us. Summing–up the situation in a split second, we executed an 'about turn' an army drill squad would have been proud of and quickly returned to the fork in the track which had been missed by our esteemed leader. There, assorted muscles were relaxed as we made our way to the nearby road, and the large signs advertising the Foreign Legion outpost nearby.

Our leader had earlier reconnoitred parts of the route but missed the need to avoid an organization not known for its benevolence to intruders.

Thereafter, it should have been plain sailing but to adapt a phrase by Oscar Wilde, to have one encounter with the Legion is unfortunate, to have two is downright careless.

Before that happened, we found that the military were not the only ones carrying guns in this area. One of the 'dips' in our route was a pass between two massive valleys which stretched down to the coast on each side of the island. It was an appropriate spot for a rest break so I whipped out my binoculars to make the most of it.

Joined by three of the group, there was a cryptic reference to the absence of vultures at which point, as luck would have it, I spotted one coming up the valley. The bird in question was a Bearded Vulture which came in low over the pass, allowing an eyeball view. It had a three metre wingspan, an orange body and a moustache Merve Hughes might be proud of. I found I was alone to admire this stunning creature; an endangered species. Both it and I were in luck that day.

For me, a week of sweat and toil was redeemed in that magical moment. As for the bird, I could only hope it never returned to the pass, littered as it was with three hundred shotgun cartridge cases. My colleagues were all convinced I'd been in harms-way and one, a chippy by trade, described this miracle of evolution, using imperial units, as 'like and eight by two batten'! I could only shake my head in wonder at his description; no appreciation for the beautiful things in life.

Next day, we were off by 6 am, making the most of the cool morning for what we knew would be a long sector. Unfortunately, it got even longer when we had to detour into the valley prematurely, as an avalanche had destroyed the track which ran along the side of a sharp ridge. By late afternoon, guys were falling down the slope, partly exhausted and partly asleep and we then ran into an apparently impenetrable wall of Alder scrub, like a head-high mixture of 'Fagus and Horizontal in Tasmania. In the true Australian sense of the word, we were bushed. However we eventually heard sheep bells again and with the aid of the binoculars, saw a shepherd boy over on the facing slope. By a miracle of communication, between shouts from our tour leader and inspired understanding from the boy, he soon appeared out of the scrub, ready to lead us down.

He slipped between the branches with ease while for us, it was a case of two steps forward ... Encumbered by our High Pack frame rucksacks, we would seem to make progress but then branches, snagged on the frame slewed us sideways or dumped us onto increasingly sore derrieres. After half-an-hour of this undignified descent, we made it to a grassy slope and reached his accommodation where mum and dad were in residence, albeit temporarily.

The last time I had seen a dwelling of this type was at Skara Brae on the Orkneys; crude, dry-stone domed structures with a turf roof, dating from 2000 BC. Here, they were the summer residence for members of farming families making the most of the Alpine summer pastures; a centuries-old way of life throughout the region.

With a ceiling clearance of little over 1.5 metres and no windows or artificial light, the fittings within were hard to ascertain. What I could see was two glowing sticks below a coffee pot and a stone sleeping bench with a blanket on the far side of the earth floor.

We had been on the march for almost twelve hours and were visibly worse for wear so they didn't hesitate to offer us their only visible food in the form of a tray of nectarines. One each only left a couple, eyed with envy but also restraint. It was without doubt, the tastiest nectarine I've ever had. Probably due to a combination of our desperation and a heritage variety, either way I was duly grateful and set-to to lay a fire across on the steep slope in the last hours of daylight. We just had time for a meal, throwing the utensils into the bracken and then it was into the bags for instant sleep.

In the morning, refreshed by our daily dose of porridge, it was time to bid our hosts farewell, a whip-round contriving to leave some francs hidden under a bar of chocolate as pathetic thanks for their hospitality. Nothing was going to compensate them for a resupply trip to the valley, 1,000 metres below, but hopefully it was the thought that counted.

Later in the trip we came across a larger, more austere version of this structure on the approaches to Paglia Orba, a peak of 2,400 metres but with a cave going through it, like a giant polo mint, half-set in the ground. This dwelling was above the grass/tree line and included a second roofless chamber for the pack horses, the location dictated by access to clean water. OK to find on a clear day but perfectly camouflaged on the rocky slopes in misty conditions. With hindsight, I feel privileged to have seen what is a vanishing way-of-life, later generations apparently preferring to service the tourist trade on the coastal strip. Easily said as long as you're not the one, alone with the sheep and the elements for months at a time.

The next food depot had been placed by Tom, our leader, at the beautiful Lac de Melo, situated in an amphitheatre of rocky peaks. Sadly when we got there, the cupboard was bare, stolen by villagers, other walkers or our prime candidate, the Legion. Who knows?

The result was a split in the party. Half descended to the valley to resupply for the long stretch ahead while the rest of us endured an anxious wait, sustained by 2 tea bags and a handful of currants. Thankfully, the heroes returned at dusk for a hurried meal, limited as much by the lack of fuel as the available daylight.

It dawned bright after another damp night and we faced the prospect of a severe climb of 500m to a ridge capped with spires. Setting off, our good spirits didn't last as we had to cross large patches of steep, hard-packed snow. An ice-axe would have come in handy; just our bad luck that the summer thaw was late that year.

We made it to the top and charged down the far side whereupon it started to rain, to such an extent that Tom crossed one creek on stepping stones above water and our tail-end Charlie had to find them under 2cm of water. The prospect of another wet night did nothing for morale as we headed into the stunted oaks but after an hour, the sun came out and a miracle occurred.

Stepping out of a belt of trees onto a fine grassy sward, we faced a mirage in the form of an Alpine Refuge Hut which wasn't marked on the map.

The hut (now one of a network along the route) could sleep 12 and had a gas stove, so morale went through the roof as we dried-out our kit and had the luxury of a meal, seated on real benches instead of unfriendly rocks.

At dusk, we had the place to ourselves but there was a late arrival in the form of a wiry, apparently hard-as-nails officer of our favourite military unit.

Determined to get a good night's sleep away from potential snorers, three of us elected to maintain the group's image and slept outside, preferring to risk wild pigs rather than any micro-wildlife occupying the hut.

In the morning we made our usual breakfast of porridge with a handful of currants thrown in. Each day, we also livened it up with a choice of powdered dessert mixes, either apple or raspberry. This was a raspberry day so we were doling out a black-spotted pink mass into our mess tins when Monsieur Legionnaire came out of the bunkroom. In the spirit of fraternity, we offered him some of this nutritious delicacy. He took one look, visibly gagged and threw us his orange and baguette, muttering deprecations about L'Écosse as he charged out of the door.

Not such a hard man after all apparently; and couldn't he see we were English? My segment of orange was delicious and porridge on sliced baguette was a welcome change, so my last encounter with the Legion proved to be another highlight of the trip.

Part 3:

FIRST

Experiences

Struggle in
the Darkness

Maggie Rose Carr

She walked slowly, carefully, the white cane searching for the next step.

The familiar smell of fresh baked bread wafted through the door of the bakery. It jogged a memory of pastries sitting in neat rows in the display counter, and of the baker's cheeky smile as he offered her a sample of one of his new delights. She knew there would be a line up, waiting to be served with the best cakes in town.

The swishing of the road sweeper, clearing last night's rubbish, joined in with the chorus of traffic as it whizzed past. A train screeched to a halt at the station, dutifully swapping its passengers before it continued on its journey. The excited squeals and laughter from children playing in the park, swirled around to find their place amongst the symphony of sound. Birds chirped noisily in the trees above, sprinkling staccato into the mix.

Making her way to the end of the path, she stopped. The blipping of the *'don't walk'* sound warned her not to cross. She had trained for this, many times. Press the button, listen, wait for the change, proceed carefully, don't hesitate. But that was with help, now there was none, just herself – alone.

OK, do this, just do it. Courage. Ah courage. A word used so freely by others. For her it was elusive, disappearing into the black. It deserted her.

She turned and walked away, back past the bakery, following the path till she reached the steps that led their way to the street above. They were familiar, comfortable. Placing her hand on the railing she ascended confidently, tapping at each step until she reached the top.

A young voice spoke to her. "Are you blind lady?"

She sensed that more than her simple – "Yes," had been expected. How many times were people going to ask this? Wasn't it obvious? Discussions about her predicament were not welcome. She did not need reminders.

Waiting for the sound of footsteps to leave, she continued on her way. Rain was coming. The coolness of the air stroked her bare shoulders, the warmth of the sun now squashed. The wind urged the rustling of leaves and stirred up the smell of fumes from vehicles urgent to deliver their occupants to their destinations.

Better hurry, no raincoat. Going home with wet hair and having to change clothes would have been an effort. Then the arduous task of getting stuff dry, hanging it on the line without dropping the pegs.

She quickened the pace slightly, mindful of the cracks that littered the pathway to her house.

Safe now, back home, in her room, she knew every corner, every niche. Once her special haven. It was different now. Now just a necessary respite from the outside world. The gentle pitter pat of rain falling on the roof, incited the gleeful memories of her childhood and 'rain drop fairies' dancing on the pathway. Fairies that now danced only in her mind.

Smoothing her hand across her bed, she reminisced the colors of the quilt, bright and cheerful. It matched the curtains, now permanently closed. Why would they need to be opened?

Carefully extracting one of the pencils from the holder on her desk, she rolled it around in her hand. The holder was handmade by her little cousin. He had been so excited, anticipating the drawing she promised him of his new puppy. The promise now meaningless.

A lamp sat on a table by her bed, never again expecting a change of globe. She wanted to keep it. It was a present from her best friend. Now gone. Taken away with her sight. Taken into the abyss. Taken by a selfish act, a careless thought, a hideous oversight. A drunken driver coming around the bend.

Bitterness was her friend now.

Voices told her – *"let it go, you have to let it go."*

But how? How could she find a way to survive this, to get used to this? Sitting down quietly on the bed, she affirmed to herself – *Tomorrow, I will do it. I will cross that road!*

The night came and she dreamt. Ah yes, dreams; people, faces, things, color, still alive in her dreams.

The ring of the alarm clock near the bed scolded that she had slept in, she usually was up before it, reminding her that a new day was beginning. Stumbling out of bed, she momentarily forgot that she could no longer see. It was happening even after a year of darkness.

Picking up her cane, she made her way to the kitchen. Listening to the slosh of water filling the kettle had taken lots of practice. A task now mastered.

Taking the milk from the fridge she carefully poured a little into her cup. Two seconds was enough poured slowly.

Milk no longer covered the table and the floor. She was getting better at this. Her toaster was adjusted just so, for toast the way she liked it. Washing up was a bit trickier, sliding her hands across plates and inside cups to make sure they were clean.

The rain had been short lived. The morning was fresh. She dressed and stepped outside into the garden.

Spring. How she had once relished it. The daffodils popping their heads above the soil to say hello to the sun. The colors of the roses and the sunlight streaming through the boughs of the large oak guarding the gate. The grass glistening from the dew of the night before, as it weaved its way beside the cobbled path. Now all just a mental photograph.

The roses would now be in full bloom. Waiting for her to feel their soft petals. *Ouch, a thorn. Damn, damn, damn, I so hate this.* She wanted to scream, to seek out that devil and punch him out. Why is he still OK? Why couldn't he die?

Making her way back into the house, she started to cry; despite all the self-promises that she would not feel sorry for herself. She was alive. Her friend wasn't.

OK, better get on with it. No time to get sorrowful now. Have to get this done.

She gently touched the lamp and made her way carefully to the front door, continued on down the steps to the street below, back again past the bakery and then ... then ...there it was – the last test.

Courage. Courage. I will do this. I will cross this road. Taking a deep breath, she waited and listened. The blip beckoned – safe to cross.

Cautiously she put her cane out in front and tapped before each step. Each step a challenge mastered. Each step a step closer to forgiveness. The other side was there. Just in front of the last tap. Stepping up onto the path she breathed the biggest sigh.

"Made it, I made it!"

A crowd had gathered from the bakery – she did not know. And then the clapping started. They had been watching, making sure she was OK.

Tears streamed down her face. She was on her way. On her way to a new life.

First Day in a New World

Meg Boland

It was not only my first trip overseas; it was my first trip on a plane and we were about to put down in Jakarta. My new frock was made of a soft material, pale blue with small puffed sleeves, and it was very, very short. I had bought it in Brisbane to impress the new family. It was soft fabric and colour but brief enough to satisfy sixties fashion canons. I had also had my hair cut short – I had asked the hairdresser to cut it as short as Mia Farrow's in *Rosemary's Baby*. I was a self-conscious token of Brisbane style.

As we stepped from the door of the plane I was bombarded by the sights, sounds and smells of a new, unimagined world. The sun beat down on my shorn and unprotected head as though the gods were stoking a furnace in the sky. And like some evil sister of the sun the humidity enfolded me. There was no nice, cool tunnel from plane to terminal but a lengthy walk across the tarmac in this blistering heat. The sweat started to pour down my face and body, even through my hair. I knew my face would be getting red, not to mention my clothes sticking to me. So much for a stylish arrival.

I was halfway to the terminal before I noticed the smell. The first hit was, surprisingly, nutmeg. I wasn't conscious of how apt it was that the first smell I had of the erstwhile 'Spice Islands' was a spice. I realised later that it was the smoke from kretek cigarettes, laced with nutmeg, perfusing the air day and night. Underneath the nutmeg smoke was the smell of the tropics, a miasma such I had never smelled before, rich and mouldy: the smell of rotting vegetation mingled with sewerage, sweat, and the sweet scent of mangoes.

We entered the dusk of the terminal. The air was still moist but at least the sun's heat had abated. There was a small altercation with the uniformed, armed customs officer. He claimed that the ham, a Christmas present for the family, was possibly a disguised gun, an argument resolved by the judicious handover of a carton of cigarettes. It was only in the entry hall that I noticed quite how many uniformed, armed men stood about. This became a motif of my stay in Indonesia at that time. Only five years after the coup that ultimately overthrew President Sukarno, the military were the dominant symbol, soldiers with guns on every other corner. But before I could notice more, we were drowned by a noisy, hugging, beaming crush of people. I had joined the family. There must have been more than a dozen of them. A young woman with a baby, two older women dressed in *sarong-kebaya* (my mother-in-law and her sister, as I was to discover), two young men and two older men smoking *kretek*, and others I wouldn't place until much later. And they all laughed and clamoured at once, in a language I had heard only rarely. The din was stupefying. I felt as though, rather than walking on my own feet, I was carried with the luggage out to the family cars. We were ensconced in Uncle John and Aunty Rose's tiny Fiat, leaving the rest of the family and the luggage to other cars.

I thought that we would never make it home. Our tiny car would inevitably be crushed and lost among the hordes of vehicles, people, animals. There were cars, buses and trucks, motor scooters, small horses with carts, minibuses, their roofs piled high with luggage, and snaking through the melee, *betjak* – trishaws carrying their passengers, alarmingly, on the front facing the chaos. Through it all were pedestrians weaving between the vehicles, intent on their various destinations, taking only perfunctory notice of the horns and klaxons of the vehicles. This was my introduction to travel in this country.

It would be two weeks before I worked out which was the 'right' side of the road for traffic. Meanwhile, I suppressed the impulse to scream: 'Watch out!' every few minutes. I closed my eyes when disaster seemed inevitable. And through the hour-long trip my husband, his aunt and his uncle talked and laughed, impervious to the danger.

Of course, we did make it home, a small stucco house in a street of small stucco houses behind the National Museum. The women of the family organised the arrival. The baby was placed in one room in the middle of an enormous bed and left

142

in the charge of her 'amah'. When it was noticed that I was wilting, I was placed in another room on another enormous bed and left gloriously alone. Despite the buzz in my head and the disarray of my senses, I attempted to doze.

I was aroused sometime later by the most unsettling cacophony I had ever heard in my life. It pervaded every corner. The Muslim call to prayer, as I discovered later, was broadcast five times a day from the national mosque near the museum and I later grew to look forward to its rhythmic cries echoing over all else. Eventually it died away and I relaxed, conscious only of the low hum of the city and my new family, still talking, catching up on three years of separation.

I became aware of a new noise in the street. A click-clack-click-clack accompanied by a hoarse cry. I sat on the side of the bed and savoured this new pattern of sound. I found out later that the musical clacking proclaimed the noodle-man with his shoulder yoke, carrying on one end a box of ingredients, noodles and its condiments, and on the other a kerosene tin with his spirit stove and wok to cook the noodles with garlic and soy sauce and some green vegetable.

Over the coming months, amid a sea of strange foods, I welcomed the click-clack of the noodle-man bringing his little kitchen at all times of day or night, with a bowl of hot noodles, no spices and no chili, no strange meat or vegetables, just warm comfort.

When I finally rose and went to join the family, Hertha, my sister-in-law, mother of the baby, fussed around me. They were all so kind and obviously asking after my welfare. But I could not understand them let alone answer them.

My new husband, in the sheer exuberance of being once again amongst his kin, seemed to have forgotten all his English. It was left to his gentle old Uncle Bie to help me out. His English was almost perfect. Beautiful. Much later I asked him how he'd learnt it. He told me that initially he had learnt from books, taught himself. There was no one to help except for the teenage son of the owners of Toko Lily down the street who was learning English at school. So, he listened to Radio Australia, night after night, month after month, year after year. He now smiled and thanked me for this opportunity to practice.

He asked Hertha to introduce me to the bath so I could feel cool and fresh before dinner. It was a huge stone vessel full of cold water. Hertha pantomimed how I was to stand beside the bath, soap myself and, using a small plastic bucket, slosh myself down with water. I gasped with the first burst of cold water against my hot skin. But then it was wonderful. The coolest and most energised I'd felt since the plane set us down. In fresh crisp clothes and feeling alive I joined the family. They were still all talking, sometimes one at a time, but often many at once, over each other. In Indonesian.

In the next couple of months, I learnt a lot of Indonesian, *melayu pasar*, market Malay, the language of the market, the shops, the kitchen, and the small private areas where the women gathered to sew and gossip. I could select food at restaurants, talk to mothers about their children, discuss family relationships, make enquiries about recipes and their ingredients, and ask the price of batik in the market, a limited but important vocabulary. I could answer the innumerable questions about my own family, my parents and siblings, about what we cooked for family meals, what I was studying. But on this first night I was all at sea, in a fog of unknowing.

We sat in the living room until it was time for dinner and the baby was passed from lap to lap, my husband's teenage brothers as well as older uncles and aunties all taking turn in playing with her. In all my times in Indonesia I never saw a baby put down unless they were asleep. There appeared to be an inexhaustible supply of friends and relatives to hold and entertain them. The family continued their cheerful exchanges and I sat smiling nicely, nibbling on peanuts and sipping iced tea. When it was time, we settled ourselves around an enormous table.

Much later I realised what a feast had been prepared for this homecoming, favourite foods from all the celebrations of the year. There was belly pork in a glistening black sauce, a large fish fried and blanketed in a glossy sweet and sour sauce, tofu stuffed with pork mince and fried, golden fried rice and fried noodles, chilies cooked whole in bean sauce, side dishes of noodle soup, spring rolls, plates of deep-fried wonton, sambal, greens, and steaming mounds of white rice. Days of work by the women of the family. And taking pride of place, on a large platter placed directly in front of me, my husband's favourite dish, a*jam goreng kuning,* yellow fried chicken. It was a whole chicken, opened flat and fried whole with a coating of garlic, turmeric, many other spices and shredded coconut. It still had its neck and head and comb attached and it was looking directly at me. All of a sudden, and quite unwittingly, all the sights and smells and sounds of the day, all the new and strange experiences, came at me in a rush, and I sat looking at that alien chicken with tears running down my face.

The Place
We Call Home

John Franks

For me, the 1992 Mabo native land title decision and now, the acknowledgement of *Prior custodianship,* and *Welcome to Country,* which we hear at meetings and events, has been something of a challenge.

It took a while for the words of the prior custodianship and Welcome to Country to sink in, as it had with the Mabo decision. Something about it was deeply disturbing to me. Was I being told that the house my parents had saved for and built and maintained, really belonged to someone else? I felt a sense of outrage, but also a desire to understand what the apparently prior claim to ownership was really about.

Up until I was five years of age, because of the building shortages after WWII, Mum, Dad, my two older sisters and I lived in a dilapidated, pest-ridden old shop building in the western suburbs of Sydney. After my parents scraped together the deposit for a block of land in the early 1950s, they borrowed from the bank to have a two-bedroom fibro and tile house built. That was the family home for fifty years. I witnessed the joy and pride my parents displayed on an almost daily basis, their pride in having their own home. It was the place where we ate, slept, played, welcomed visitors, celebrated birthdays and Christmas, and grew up.

My first awakening came in my early twenties, when I read Xavier Herbert's, *Poor Fellow My Country;* all 1563 pages of it. It made such an impact, I read it again a couple of years later after I had been posted to a country town with a significant Aboriginal population. As a young 'white' school pupil I had been taught how 'Captain' Cook discovered Australia: WRONG! I later experienced the transition from *God Save the Queen* to the original wording of Advance Australia Fair: WRONG! We weren't all able to rejoice to the same extent. As a teacher, I have taught how explorers and early settlers discovered and settled new lands with only minor disputes and violence: WRONG! The most damaging error in this whole sorry saga had been made by James Cook in 1770 when he claimed *Terra Australis* for England based on *Terra Nullius*: WRONG!

The land was not unoccupied, and hadn't been for over 50,000 years. In 1992, after numerous unsuccessful battles in the Supreme and High Courts of Australia, the momentous Mabo case finally acknowledged the history of dispossession of First Nations people of their land, thereby abolishing the legal fiction of *Terra Nullius,* and altered the fundamentals of Australian land law. In 1996, the decision in the case mounted by the Wik people in the Supreme Court succeeded in acknowledging that native title could coexist with, and was not extinguished by, pastoral leases.

In my book *Memoirs (warts and all) of a Baby Boomer,* I wrote of two events of lasting impression. The first was when we had been 'bush-bashing' in the Northern Territory. At Palm Valley, I had recognised Charles Perkins, a powerful and outspoken voice for Aboriginal Rights and the instigator of the 'Freedom Ride' bus journeys to draw public attention to the poor state of Aboriginal health, education and housing. I didn't speak to him then but two days later, while we were sitting in the Stuart Arms Hotel in Alice Springs, he walked in with his delegation. I asked him if he had also visited Hermannsburg Mission where we had had something of a misadventure, which I thought I might tell him about. Twenty minutes after my initial question he stopped to draw breath, having given his damning assessment of how much damage the missionaries had done to Aboriginal peoples. I never did get to tell him my story.

I have mentioned previously some difficulties in teaching in a town which Perkins would have passed through, with an itinerant Aboriginal population. While working there I could have been more outspoken about inequalities but, like so many of us, I chose the path of least resistance and said very little.

The second event described how a mate and I were virtually bailed up on the Stuart Highway by a small clan of perhaps twenty Aborigines. It was about 9:30pm, New Year's Eve, 1975 and we adopted the attitude of those times, "peace brother" (we were later told that they were heading for a tribal reunion. A corroboree?). No harm was done to anyone other than my nervous system while driving in fear that one of them was going to fall off the roof-rack of our Nissan Patrol they were hanging on to.

The history of dispossession and colonisation lies at the heart of the disparity between Aborigines and Torres Strait Islanders and non-indigenous Australians today. Now in my senior years, I recognise the main cause: *un-truthfulness*, from the classroom to government policy and society in general. These days I try to improve my understanding of what might work to improve race relations in Australia. Recent books which have helped to understand the extent of the problem. *Denny Day*, an outstanding book by Terry Smyth tells the story of how Andrew Denny Day, was a police magistrate who tracked down the perpetrators of the infamous Myall Creek massacre near Bingara, NSW on June 10th, 1838. Twenty-eight innocent men, women and children were shot dead. That was only one of what is now judged to be at least 400 massacres of Aborigines Australia wide. Another book, *The Secret River* by Kate Grenville explores the clashes between Europeans and Aborigines as the 'settlers' took over tribal lands by force. Similar themes are explored from an Aboriginal perspective by Julie Janson in *Benevolence*. That story is of a Dharug woman experiencing first contact with Europeans and the impact of British colonisation resulting in cataclysmic changes accompanied by violence, sickness and starvation.

Aboriginal and Torres Strait Islander peoples have experienced a long history of exclusion from Australian history books, the national flag, the national anthem and, for many years, Australian democracy. All perpetrated by the false narrative purveyed in our education systems over generations.

Recognition of Aboriginal and Torres Strait Islander peoples in events, meetings and functions recognise in a small way the exclusion that has been so damaging. We are reminded of their existence, past and present.

Incorporating welcome and acknowledgement protocols into official meetings and events respectfully recognises Aboriginal and Torres Strait Islander peoples as the traditional owners of the land. As Professor Mick Dodson has said, "Aboriginal people may no longer necessarily be the title-holders to land, but they are still connected to the Country of their ancestors and most consider themselves the custodians or caretakers of their land."

The Uluru Statement from the Heart speaks to us all: "*We Aboriginal nations, were the first sovereign Nations of the Australian continent and its adjacent islands, and possessed it under our own laws and customs for more than 60,000 years.*

We call for the establishment of a First Nations Voice enshrined in the Constitution. 'Makarrata' may be defined as, the coming together after a struggle. It captures our aspirations for a fair and truthful relationship with the people of Australia and a better future for our children based on justice and self-determination.

We seek a Makarrata Commission to supervise a process of agreement-making between governments and First Nations and truth-telling about our history.

In 1967 we were counted, now, in 2017, we seek to be heard. We invite you to walk with us in a movement of the Australian people for a better future."

My parents are no longer with us, but the memories of those formative years of our family living in our fibro and tile castle are indelibly etched in our family history. To that extent, I share that love of place and the places we all call home.

First Flight

Diana Souter

A deafening, terrifying whine screamed overhead, banking towards the sea, then thinking better of it, spun around and made for home. Home was Williamtown airbase and amid much fanfare, the shiny new F35A Joint Strike Fighter planes had arrived at Port Stephens. They were to be Australia's first line of defence, a guardian of our skies against unwanted intruders. I watched it fade into the distance from my balcony and quite suddenly, as the mind does unbidden sometimes, remembered another flying machine at another place and another more peaceful time: my first overseas flight.

In those long-ago days of my youth in the 1960s, traveling by air was an expensive and glamorous affair. No-one we knew had even been in a plane let alone abroad, and I was the first in the whole extended family to travel around the world in 1964. Was this then the start of my love affair with that opulent airborne taxi?

My first flying adventure occurred, however, earlier in 1962 when I went from teaching in the second hottest furthest west school in NSW to the second most easterly school after Norfolk – Lord Howe Island. This was a two-teacher school set in a world heritage listed paradise with magnificent beaches, tangled jungles, pristine clear waters and coral atolls.

It had only one drawback: the only way to get there was by ship from Sydney or New Zealand or by a Sunderland Flying Boat. It sported four engines (two on each wing) a veritable double decker bus with wings, complete with floaters to land on the water in the lagoon. The upstairs section was decked out as a lounge with cocktails served with panache by a glamorous young hostess.

Imagine my excitement at boarding this exotic craft at age twenty. I felt like a celebrity, wearing my sweet, pale blue suit with short skirt, matching earrings and hand bag. When we took off from Rose Bay in Sydney, having drinkies and flirting with the captain, I felt so romantic and grown up!

There were only two of these magnificent craft left then, many having been lost in Europe during the last war. The flying boat serviced the island once or twice a week, with their landings carefully timed to coincide with the tides. Sometimes it would break down or be late, or miss the tide, disappointing holiday makers eager to visit and locals eager for their mail and goods ordered from the mainland. It was also captive to good weather, gliding serenely on to the turquoise waters of the lagoon in between the coral reef and wild deep blue ocean.

My young heart would skip a beat each time it landed, as I ran to the jetty to see if my handsome pilot friend would be on it, having met him on my flights home at the end of each school term. The crew: pilot, engineer and hostess stayed the night, and were royally entertained by the local hostelries.

As my tenure was for two years, I boarded with Mr and Mrs King, whose ancestors could be traced back to the infamous 'Mutiny on the Bounty'. Philip Gidley King was the third governor of New South Wales from 1800 to 1806. He also went on to set up the penal colony at Norfolk Island. Whilst enroute to Tahiti to gather saplings from the Breadfruit Tree, the crew mutinied, with some survivors jumping ship at Pitcairn.

Some of the children at Lord Howe were descended from survivors of that ill-fated trip in 1787. One of my pupils Rosanne looked like a Polynesian princess, with her dark eyes and glossy long crinkly black hair. Lord Howe is now known for its relaxing holiday resorts, lovely indoor palm tree industry as well as pristine coral diving adventures, after all that violence.

This was a two-teacher school, with the headmaster taking classes for students aged from nine to twelve, and I took the littlies aged four to eight. Living on a tropical paradise was idyllic, if a little restricted. My free time was filled with listening to records bought from the Readers Digest by post, playing tennis, choosing clothes ordered from the David Jones catalogue, painting scenes and collecting shells. Later, I would begin to plan my first world trip, with this sojourn giving me a taste for even more adventure. I learnt to water ski, partied with gusto and invited famous people there on holiday to the school to speak to the kiddies. Whilst walking carefully to school through jungle and dodging spiders as large as saucers, I marvelled at my good fortune at being chosen for this job.

At twenty, I fell in love with a dashing local, who was in the Merchant Navy. Word soon spread, as a courtship done in secrecy was impossible, of course, as in such a small community of only three-hundred people, as gossip was then today's Facebook. However, it wasn't all moonlight and roses, as one fateful night I awoke to the sound of a tin roof slicing through a palm tree, the wind screaming and felling swathes of jungle, with the rain lashing outside my window. Terrified, I imagined with horror the scene unfolding below my hill on the shore. On this unforgettable night in a violent tropical storm, a tethered flying boat broke its moorings and ended up battered and broken on the local beach.

"... *it was carrying a happy band of bowlers enroute from Sydney to Noumea. During the dark early hours came the storm, high winds and heavy seas, the flying boat broke its moorings and flung itself up on to Lagoon Beach. One wing buried itself in the sand and its float smashed. In wind and rain and bitter cold, the intrepid islanders rallying to an emergency as always managed to upright her. With men and tractors pushing and pulling, the one working engine full blast, she slipped back into the water, men sitting on the wings, boats pushing and heaving and smashing on to the coral. Alas one engine was ruined by sand and water; nothing could be done to save her."*

What an historical event to witness! My report published in the Sydney Morning Herald "Death of a Chieftain" (The plane's name was Pacific Chieftain), earned me a reprimand from Sir Reginald Ansett himself! Later, a 'wake' was held as they stripped her of oil, engines and furniture. At that time, we were isolated. Luckily, there was one other 'Beachcomber' available to carry on the service for another couple of years, but sadly the flying boat service doesn't exist anymore.

There is an airfield there now, with small Qantas planes landing three times per week, but where's the romance in that? Yes, flying then was certainly an adventure and a far cry from today's speedy luxurious silver torpedos. So, as the new shiny deadly fighter planes roared over my head, flinging themselves into the distance, their roar slowly fading, I pulled myself back to the present and gave thanks for those clever, brave and courageous men and women in their flying machines – in air or over water.

Yes, history and progress march on, and unfortunately it was on March 2002 that the final Ansett Airlines flight took place. Founded by Sir Reginald in 1935, Ansett had been our biggest domestic airline for seven decades and having often flown with them myself, I was sad to see it go. My final homage was to attend an auction in Sydney of some of its plane's fittings, so that now I savour my breakfast boiled egg from an Ansett egg cup. Today there are dozens of local and international airlines flying in Australia to and from all over the world, but I will never again feel the thrill of that first flying floating machine and the time that left me bereft at the death of a Chieftain.

Mr Mitchell

Lorraine James

The first day at school is never good. I know this because I experienced a number of them. Holding onto Mummy's hand, reluctantly letting go when she leaves and turns back to wave with a teary smile that is meant to be reassuring, but fails miserably.

In New Zealand in the 1940s, before I turned eight years old, we moved around a lot because of my father's job. Up until the age of five I was an only child and because, due to World War II when our lives were rather transitory, I didn't have friends to play with. I was a loner but not lonely as I invented an imaginary friend, Ann, who became the bane of my mother's existence for several years.

I started school during World War II when I was five and my mother and I were living with my grandmother in Auckland because Dad had been called up to fight in the Pacific. I was enrolled at the nearest primary school. It was two miles from home and I walked. I remember the route to this day – the houses, the grey stone walls with tiny purple flowers sprouting out of the cracks. The black bitumen pavements were dotted with little fragments of white sparkly shell and the surface, during hot days, melted in places and became soft. Along the way I would circumnavigate some playing fields. Behind them was a hill with a derelict windmill on the top. Occasionally I'd take a detour on the way home and climb up to study it closely.

The school was an experimental school in that children were assessed, not only according to their IQ and learning abilities but also for any special skill they might have. Once that was established they were encouraged to advance that propensity and my particular skills were deemed singing and writing stories.

A few weeks after I started school, as was customary, Mum was given an appointment with the headmistress, Mrs Gilbert. She asked how I was liking school and Mum told her that I seemed to be happy – the only thing I didn't enjoy was morning assembly. This took place in the playground when the weather was fine. The whole school would assemble, we would sing the national anthem while the New Zealand flag was raised and the headmistress would talk to us about things to do with school events. Mrs Gilbert was interested to know why I didn't like this part of the day and Mum told her that I said it was too crowded.

"Well, that's easy to fix," said Mrs G. Lillian can always stand at the end of the row." So I did.

The school had a series of identical buildings with two classrooms in each. They were built in the distinctive New Zealand style of the day

– timber, painted white. They had lovely big windows and the classrooms were very bright and cheerful. There were extensive grass playing fields for rugby and cricket. In one corner of the grounds was a little dental clinic built in a miniature style to match the rest of the buildings. It was known as 'The Murder House'. There were low grey stone walls surrounding the school grounds with shady trees under which the milk crates would be stacked up at the gate. New Zealand provided free milk and dental services to all schools. The milk was in half pint glass bottles sealed with a cardboard lid with a hole that you punctured with a straw. In the summer the milk was warm and revolting with the cream risen to the top.

I would guess that I was only at that first school for a year because when my father came home after the Pacific War ended, we went back to Wellington and Dad returned to his job. During that time, we lived in two houses. I hated the school located in Naenae, while the second one at Eastbourne in The Bays, I loved. Some fifty years later when I was visiting friends who were giving a dinner party and lived in The Bays, one of the guests, when we were introduced, said "I know you" and produced a primary school class photo with both of us in it.

"When there was no teacher available to teach our class, you were always chosen to keep the class in check," he said.

I have no memory of this but apparently, after the war there was such a shortage of teachers that at times it was common for none to be available as they had to spread themselves between classes.

I was seven years old and can only suspect that I was 'The Chosen One' because, perhaps ... was I the bossiest?

My father decided he wanted to start his own business and so we packed up again and went back to Auckland and I returned to my first school. I was academically assessed and placed in 'A' class.

On my first morning I walked into a class of children, who were already well settled in. The teacher, Mr Mitchell, said in the friendliest and most welcoming way "Hello Tootsie!" to which I haughtily replied; "My name is Lillian Katherine Finn".

"That's right Tootsie," said Mr Mitchell, immediately cutting me down to size. "You sit over there."

He called me Tootsie from then on except during official moments, for example when he was conducting the morning role call or announcing the weekly test results or if I was in trouble, which was inevitably when I hadn't done well in maths. But I've always figured that (before the advent of the calculator) if I could add, subtract, divide and multiply, I'd get on fine, and I have.

In the behaviour department I never got into trouble. I was the ultimate 'Miss Goody Goody'.

What a gift I was given with Ray Mitchell. Mr Mitchell was a slim man of medium height – immaculately groomed with dark hair, nice looking, and he smiled readily. He had quite sharp features with a straight narrow nose. In the manner of the day, he always wore a shirt and tie, lovely tweed wool sports jackets and very shiny brown shoes.

He eventually was promoted to headmaster in other schools but when I joined him, he was teaching a class of eight, nine and ten year old students. The school had a system, whereby children were graded academically and stayed with the same teacher for three years after which they left the primary school and moved to an intermediate school. They would then spend two years in preparation for secondary school.

We all loved him. He was strict but fair. He was kind, warm, fun, inventive, interesting, had a great sense of humour – everything any kid would want in a teacher. I can imagine he would go home in the evenings with humorous stories about his class as we were, after all, just little children and probably very funny at times.

We were all so proud to be in his class and our greatest fear was the possibility of being downgraded to Class B: Miss Parson's class. Miss P was a perfectly lovely teacher but 'B' class? Humiliation!

My best friend (Julie Morrison) and I must have been slacking off at some stage because one Monday we arrived at school and were told to pack our school bags, which were leather and heavy in those days. We were then told to sit on the little platform that ran along the front of the classroom beneath the blackboard. Perhaps we had been getting poor marks in our weekly tests, which were held on Fridays and then on Monday morning.

Upon arrival in the class, the results would be read out and the students would then be moved to sit in a row according to their test results. Front row were the top performers. Back row the worst.

Julie and I sat on the platform and snivelled away, devastated to think that we might be 'sent down' to Miss Parson's class. Last minute reprieve.

"Righto you two," Mr Mitchell said. Go and sit in the back row and pull your socks up."

Obviously, we did as we never had to go through that humiliation again.

Besides developing our reading skills, creative writing and spelling, Mr Mitchell made history lessons absolutely riveting by including plenty of blood and gore to keep the boys engrossed. Good behaviour, good manners, courtesy, consideration for others, respect and many other attributes were drummed into us but we also had loads of fun. We would have 'expeditions' regularly. To the Bycroft biscuit factory. To the Tip Top ice cream factory. To the museum to learn about Maori history where we would stand in awe in front of the gigantic Moa skeleton in the massive foyer.

Mr Mitchell was kind but he did use the strap sparingly if a boy had really crossed the line. This, of course, was the forties when cultural mores were very different. In his class, girls were never punished punitively but in those days the strap was just accepted as fair punishment by school children.

Once we graduated from using pencils that we had upgraded to pens which were made of slender wood with a fine metal nib inserted at the end. We had an inkwell set into the desk to dip the pen into which, when we were beginners, resulted in lots of blots. We had blotting paper to attend to that. The ink was always blue/black in school but inks were also available in royal blue or black. I loved the smell of the ink.

One day, I must have lost my pen and Mr Mitchell lent me his fountain pen. I was so proud. It was a Parker – beautiful in mottled green and black – so smooth and tactile. I longed to have one of my own and eventually I did, once I was at intermediate school. Fountain pens had a permanent nib which, with use, adapted to the individual owner's way of writing for example, if they pressed down hard or wrote with a light hand. Although ballpoint pens had been released by Biro in 1938, they were not used in New Zealand schools in the forties.

Some time during those three years I fell in love with Tony Forrester. He was a slightly built boy with dark hair and in my opinion, extremely handsome. At one stage during this unfulfilled romance, I cycled over to his address to have a look at his house. It was in a very posh, leafy street in a very swanky suburb and was a very large and posh house which added to his allure. I don't think we ever really had a proper conversation but just admired each other from afar. One morning, I sat down at my desk, felt a sharp pain and discovered a drawing pin impaled in my bottom with 'I love you' printed in miniscule letters around the cardboard protector. The other boys in the class all swore it was Tony who had put it there and his red face did rather give him away. Ah, unrequited love!

Of course, as usual in mixed classes, the boys teased the girls and I received my fair share, notably when a boy chased me around the classroom and stabbed the back of my calf with the sharp nib of his pen. I still have that tattoo – just one little blue/ black dot.

Many children who had had the privilege of being taught by Ray Mitchell went on to succeed in life. Due to the school's policy of developing the individual potential of every child and nurturing any specific gift they might show, we all had a sense of self esteem in that we were recognized throughout the school as being good at something. One student might be renowned for his football prowess, another for his excellence in science, another in the arts. The ground work that Mr Mitchell gifted his students with, just in the three years of classes I spent with him, produced a nuclear scientist, a world-famous artist, an All Black, a member of the New Zealand cricket eleven, surgeons, barristers and others, like me, who succeeded in their own businesses.

During the time we spent with him he ensured that we left him as well adjusted, literate and responsible human beings, but above all he strove to build our characters. What we have achieved with his gift to us as our lives have progressed has been entirely up to us.

Doorway to the Unknown

Kate Mannell

The distant, echoing cry of the whales permeated the water. Surfacing to gasp in a deep breath of air, I pushed myself back under to once again find myself in that peaceful blue world. This side of the water's surface, the calm silence broken only by the whales' haunting melody, was humbling. There's working five days a week, spending hours navigating asphalt roads, wandering the supermarket aisles, going to the dentist. And then there's floating underwater off the coast of a Hawaiian island, face to face with refrigerator-sized Galapagos sharks, while whales sing in the blue depths not far away.

The first time I remember hearing whale calls was in primary school. There were about twenty of us, from kindergarten to year two, in the one of two classrooms in the small country public school just off the highway. We would stretch out on the coarse, navy carpet with multi-coloured flecks and listen. Mrs Blattman would put a CD into the stereo. The air that was silent with anticipation would fill with the high-pitched squeals and low wails of the huge ocean mammals, and we would lie still and float in the sound. I never considered that I would hear the animals firsthand, and the exotic location in which that would occur.

Almost two decades after that classroom, and two years cut off from the life I expected in my early twenties, I was able to travel again and find myself in such a wondrous place as that patch of ocean on the north-western side of O'ahu. After two years of stagnation in the grip of a pandemic, I had almost forgotten what it was like to experience the unknown. To be reminded, you are never too old to experience something for the first time. That in a world so rich in cultures, landscapes and people, there will always be something new. Travel is a passage to the unfamiliar. Many of my most significant first experiences have been outside the world I know. Sheer unfiltered beauty. Raw emotion. Violence and death. My wealth is in moments, and I would not change them for anything. Even the monumental moment of my first kiss was far off the coast of Australia – a family holiday sailing the seas on the Pacific Sun.

I was freshly eighteen when I dared to brave my first solo adventure. I'd taken some Spanish classes with a local Ecuadorian man. His lessons were more than language; they echoed his spiritual connection to his Inca ancestors and prepared me for the culture in a way no online video or travel guide could.

And it wasn't the culture shock that got to me. It was the isolation. I had never spent so long away from my family. I felt pain and loneliness unlike anything I had felt before. I cried often. I'd awake in the cold air of a tent, disorientated and believing I could hear the magpies warbling in the warm winter sun rising over the cattle-strewn hills, only to find a desolate Patagonian steppe outside the canvas flap.

The strength that comes from your lowest point started to bloom within me. I missed home with every fibre of my being, but I embraced each new day with willingness and curiosity. The strangers in my group began to feel like a family to me. Each town we passed, each moment, started to build up and fill my heart so that I did not feel alone.

There were three days in a hostel in the town of El Chalten, located within Los Glaciers National Park, where I did something I had never truly attempted before. I woke up before the sun, quietly dropping from the top bunk in a room of ten beds. The streetlights were still on, fog twirling in their beams. The first rays of the sun peeped above the eastern horizon as I set foot on the trail, its light reflecting molten pink on the western snow-capped peaks.

There was no one on the trail for as far as I could see in front of me and behind me. It was my first independent trek. And I was gloriously alone. The dirt path was barely wider than my hips in some places, worn down half a metre from the natural level of the ground. When I stopped for my first break a few kilometres in, I found that my pear had mushed into my phone, leaving me with less food than I'd anticipated. Rays of light filtered through the canopy of wooded areas along the trail, creating iridescent globes of light in the lens of my digital camera. Where the trail was downhill or flat, I breezed along at a leisurely pace. I felt strong, blissful and balanced. Where the trail sloped upwards, I tired quickly and worried I would not reach my destination. Each aspect of the landscape was different and beautiful, taking me to ridgetops overlooking wide valleys, grassy hillsides, forests of spindly trees, and jagged towering mountains. Each part of the journey was marked by different slopes. I felt as if I were experiencing life at an accelerated pace. I learned that the path undulates, and my feet would carry me on.

In the Chilean city of Santiago, I discovered beer was not for me. Locking myself in the bathroom of a random night club, with absolutely no idea of where I was as my body rejected everything in my stomach, I was terrified. This had never happened to me at parties back home. I remember the wind in my face as I hung my head from the taxi window. I remember Thomas carrying me into the hotel room. I remember feeling exposed and embarrassed as Anette stripped me of my vomit-soaked clothes and herded me into the shower. I'll never forget their kindness as they ensured I was packed and on the truck the next morning – and how my cleaned clothes were delivered to me at the next stop. While not many can say their first experience with an alcohol overdose and a major hangover was something special, the selflessness of these people who had been strangers only months before continues to be a moment I cherish.

The hyper-independence I'd adopted as I adjusted to the separation from my family, thousands of kilometres away, had a lesson in store for me. The beautiful city of Salta, Argentina, sprawled across the valley floor on which it had settled. White and terracotta-coloured buildings dotted the ground below through the city haze. I can't remember now whether a group of us had caught cable cars to the mountain top or if we had walked. I do remember thinking how beautiful the outlook would be at night.

While the rest of the tour group made dinner plans, I strode off into the early evening with my camera and determination to see the city lights. I made it to the park where the trail started. The cable cars weren't running after 7 pm, and I wanted to save money by walking up. The public park, which had been filled with picnickers and people supporting a bicycle race hours before, was now deserted and eerily quiet. The closer I drew to the stairs up the Cerro San Bernardo, the darker it became. There was no lighting along the path. The only sources of light were the moon and the city lights. I considered if I should have brought my headlamp. On the other hand, I reasoned it might be better to remain unseen than be a beacon of vulnerability. I'd ascended for about ten minutes before I realised the error of my ways. I'd become so swept up in the pride of not being afraid that I had forgotten caution.

Treading quietly down the trail, holding my breath as every noise in the dense vegetation surrounding me was amplified, I was relieved when I reached the lights of the park. But it wasn't over yet. The city looked different under the cover of night. I knew the general direction back to the hostel. It was still many blocks away when a figure began to follow me. No matter how briskly I walked, he continued to gain ground. We were not in an isolated area, but nor were there many people around either. He spoke to me in Spanish, introducing himself. I responded politely but he soon switched to English when my Spanish failed. He mentioned being a teacher and was interested to know where I was from. The conversation was fine until he started asking where my hostel was. Until we had passed too many corners for it to be 'just around the corner' as I assured him each time he asked. I avoided checking my map, pretending to be sure of where I was going.

Just as I began to run out of convincing assurances that we were 'very' close to my hostel, I came upon a welcome sight. A line of people meandered up the path on the opposite side of the street. Of all the times, on all the streets and all the people to be there at this moment in the foreign city, there they were – my friends from the tour group. With only so much as an overly excited comment on spotting my friends and a terse goodbye, I sprinted across the road, barely caring for traffic. Leaving the man on the corner. I was relieved to envelop myself in the safety of the group. Humbled and relieved.

A couple of days before my flight home, after four months of highs, lows and irrevocable life lessons, the fresh coolness of an Amazonian waterfall washed over me and my yellow gum boots. The jungle was alive in a way a bustling city never could be. We trailed our guide, Miguel, through thigh-high grasses and narrow muddy paths while dodging lush branches. The heart of the Amazon was hundreds of kilometres away yet even on the edge of such a mysterious and undiscovered place, its wildness could be felt. Channelling my inner Tarzan, I swung from a thick vine and screeched with delight as it took my weight and arced over a small depression in the forest floor. Miguel reached into the clear waters of a gently flowing creek, scooping clay from its bed and spreading it across my face. 'It will make you even more beautiful', he said with a flirtatious smile.

My journey through South America was marked by firsts, and not just in regard to the places I had never been before. It was my first time being truly alone. Interacting with strangers in a whole new capacity. Testing the limits to my resilience, bravery and naivety. Truly understanding there will always be the unwonted to see, to experience and to be in this wide, magnificent and wondrous world.

The rubber raft bounced along the churning rapids, pulled along by the mighty current. In India, the sky is rarely clear and that afternoon, even far from the main cities, was no different. The golden red sun shimmered in a brown haze as it made its descent. The brilliant misty blue glacial waters of the mighty Ganges River called to me. My wetsuit was stifling in the still heat of the day. As the roiling waters calmed, our Canadian dread-locked rafting guy who was most definitely not high, gave us the go ahead to jump in. There is something spiritual about jumping into cold water without hesitation. That split second when your lungs seem to drop to your feet and your blood forgets which way to flow. As I bobbed along on my back, I revelled in the invigorating water, and I could see why the locals used it as more than just a natural resource. It wasn't until later that evening, when our raft guide's glazed eyes stared into the fire, that he revealed that I'd shared the water with the semi-burnt remains of those who believed the sacred Ganges would purify and provide enlightenment after life.

Death is something I've been sheltered from for quite some time. It was something I never expected to see in downtown Waikiki. My brother, myself and our respective partners did a few laps of various blocks trying to decide on dinner that night. As the tourist numbers dwindled, homeless people appeared in numbers to settle in for the night under the sheltered awnings of closed shopfronts. We decided on a pizza place, which seemed to be winding up business. I began to feel unwell and suggested we take the pizzas back to the hotel room. Utterly exhausted, we all agreed.

We wandered back past the Irish pub; a sinister atmosphere brewing just outside its doors. There were a few people loitering around the large blue post box outside the pub that caught my attention. I don't remember now why. The footpath outside the pub seemed to be in darkness, as if the streetlights weren't on, and the streets that were so often alive at night were desolate. Anxious to get back to the hotel and lie down after a full-on day, I picked up the pace.

I saw the pedestrian light ahead of us transition from the walking man to the flashing raised hand, giving us thirty seconds to cross. I called to our group to hurry up, and we half jogged, half shuffled across the quiet road. We'd barely made it up the path on the other side of the road when we heard a loud pop-pop. I paused.

That muffler sounded very weird.

Wait.

There weren't many cars around.

Turning back to the corner from which we'd just crossed, we saw a crumpled form on the ground and a man beside it running in circles. 'He's been shot! He's been shot!' the man cried, dashing back and forth while waving his hands in the air

I caught sight of people running back down the street of the Irish pub, the soles of their shoes picking up the dim light as they disappeared into the shadows. The figure on the ground wasn't moving. It looked like just a dark heap of clothes.

How do you respond to something you've never experienced before? I want to say my first instinct was to run across and perform first aid. I can't even say my first instinct was to run and hide. I didn't know what to do. I didn't have a phone with a SIM card to call 911. There was a restaurant a few doors away which must have heard the shooting, a hush had descended among the diners in the outdoor area.

There would be no bloodstain on the corner when I walked past early the next morning. No sign anything had ever happened. I'd later find out that the person who was shot had died, and that the gunman was still on the loose – considered armed and dangerous. Two days after the shooting I would see a few leis wrapped around the lamppost on that corner, and a piece of paper stuck to the lamp's street sign. RIP Polo. He was only a few months older than my little brother. The next day the requiem was gone. Buskers played along the street as tourists filtered past. I would avoid that corner for the rest of the trip where I could, but by the end of the trip I would walk upon that corner without a second thought. I would walk, just like everyone else, over the place where a young man was shot dead only days before.

The time ahead is uncertain. No matter how the ground shifts beneath my feet, my wanderlust will not waver. There is clarity in discovering new places, pushing the boundaries of the familiar, and experiencing the raw and the extraordinary. While I only need to step out the door to find a first experience, travel opens a doorway unlike any other into the unknown.

Inspired

Pharaoh's Dream

John Franks

1968 - 1974

It was as if Pharaoh's dream (Genesis: Ch:41) of seven years of plenty followed by seven years of famine had been randomly merged. The good was mixed haphazardly with the not-so-good ... bad even.

Francis J Richards, FJ to his friends, completed the first ever New South Wales Higher School Certificate (HSC) in 1967. His pass in that exam, and his school reports generally, were devoid of any pretensions to high academic achievement. He was an 'also rans' of that particular race – neither a winner nor a failure. Like most boys, he was full of teenage hormones, mostly bottled up with no place to go. A teacher once told him he was precocious. Probably because he was covering up the fact that he had little or no idea what he wanted to do or be and tried to make smart comments. At the end of 1967, his school uniform hung rejected in his wardrobe, never to be worn again – unloved, unlamented, waiting for the Vinny's bag.

1968: His first full-time job. Like so many others at the time, FJ was the first in the family to stay the full course of secondary education. Not one uncle, aunt or cousin had the Leaving Certificate. Nor had any family member, or even close friend, worked at a professional level. They were mostly engaged in factory or clerical work, or retail sales.

His HSC pass attracted an invitation to join the NSW Public Service which, on his father's advice, he accepted. He had previously rejected a Teachers' College scholarship because he thought it was a step backwards into the world of education, and not having anyone with whom he could discuss opportunities or even possibilities. Vocational Guidance of the day he and his mates thought of as a joke.

In due course he reported as directed to the NSW Department of Lands, and signed up as Junior Survey Draughtsman. He enrolled in the Land and Engineering Surveying course at Sydney TAFE. From day one his enthusiasm diminished. He passed the TAFE exams, but the office work was tedious and, in his immature mind, the work just didn't appeal. In an about turn at the end of the year, he reapplied for a Teachers' College scholarship and was accepted.

1969: Acting like an adolescent. Whereas his parents had influenced his first job, becoming a teacher was all down to FJ himself. It transpired he was a dreadful college student. A year out of school had allowed him to make most of his own decisions including buying his first of fourteen motorbikes and obtaining his driving licence. More freedom allowed him to make even more thoughtless decisions, some would say, selfish. The fact that his girlfriend at that time had been appointed to Wollongong Teachers' College put an end to that relationship which affected his self-esteem.

Unexpectedly, later that year he was asked to partner a girl from a family within the parish circle, who was making her debut. It involved attending numerous rehearsals for learning dances and the protocols for the ceremony itself. After a shaky start, the relationship developed and contributed to more poor student behaviour. At the time he thought he was being so clever, missing lectures and failing to complete assignments. It made him feel 'in charge and grown-up'.

1970: Wake-up calls. By 1970, FJ knew he was treading a very thin line at teachers' college. On several occasions he was called to the principal's office to show cause to be allowed to continue. Finally, the embarrassment of being sent on his way from college made him change his ways. It wasn't a St Paul/Damascus experience. It took time, but it was a start. He had too many bad habits to shed at one go, but he knew he was the only one who could do it. PE and Music were the subjects which appealed. Art and Craft were well below the Plimsoll Line of achievement. He was in danger of foundering.

One lesson he learnt completely by accident. In happened in a music lecture. He was offered a clarinet on loan, and he immediately fell in love with it.. Unbeknown to him at the time, it was to change his focus on his goals in life. It demonstrated the bleeding obvious that if he wanted to improve, he had to work at it. It also influenced his relationship with his girlfriend, Marnie Acheron, (Not her real name but check 'Acheron' in Greek Mythology) and they became more of an 'item'. Appearances mattered, and failure wasn't a good look with her. The end of the year was approaching, and he realised that, assuming he survived until then, he would graduate as a teacher and be placed in a school somewhere in New South Wales, not of his choice.

1971: Chickens coming home to roost. Graduate he did, and in January 1971, FJ received the dreaded telegram notifying him of his appointment as temporary teacher-in-charge at 'Hazel Park Public School, Lowlands, via Bellata'. It was clear the Department of Education had the last laugh. The school was six hundred kilometres from the family home. The location wasn't on the map he bought from the local garage. Phone calls to the Department, followed by calls to the school secretary, helped him find it.

Professionally FJ was in uncharted territory, never having been away from home for more than a couple of weeks at a time, and then at predominantly supervised activities. He had to leave his friends, including his girlfriend, behind in Sydney and learn to live in a partly furnished house in an isolated scattered farming community.

To top it all, there had been a flood in the Namoi Valley region and bridges were impassable and roads were closed, as was, for the time being, the school.

After three weeks, FJ finally received news the roads were open, so he packed his car with every household item his mother thought he needed and, with a map on the seat beside him alongside his sandwiches she had prepared, he set off for his first appointment as a schoolteacher. At least six times he had to stop and confirm the directions. The last stage was managed via a fortuitous meeting with the school secretary, Max Camford, who was driving his Land Rover along the same road towards a bridge, the approaches to which had been washed out in the flood. Max took FJ, and some of his possessions to finish the journey by crossing a ford downstream of the bridge, and drove him to his homestead for a couple of days while the house for the teacher was being made habitable. That involved removing a dead and rotting kangaroo and a rumour of a snake in the house.

Every day was a new experience. The school enrolment began with seventeen students including three high school students doing correspondence, one kindergarten child and a scattering of children in other grades. FJ had zero knowledge of how to cope with the Departmental red tape awaiting him. He'd never seen a one-teacher school let alone been put in charge of one and he felt he was blundering from one day to the next.

Coincidentally, the effects of the flood and a dramatic collapse of prices in the sheep industry resulted in a few families moving away. Five months later, the Department in its wisdom, closed the school. FJ was transferred to Wee Waa Central School 70 km away to adapt to a life living in a men's teachers' hostel with six others of similar age and varied experiences, including one raw recruit from Egypt who spoke very little English..

1972: Learning curves. In the ebb and flow of life's fortunes FJ experienced the challenges of living in shared accommodation. However, hostilities never broke out although strong language contributed to the amount of paint peeling off the walls. He settled into a barely acceptable state of chaos. His steepest learning curve was to understand their different values and attitudes towards the 'little' things such as cleanliness, punctuality and sharing common facilities, food and equipment.

Later that year Marnie came to stay with him in the hostel on occasions when university breaks coincided with school holidays. She would stay for a few days after which they would drive back to Sydney. Hardly anyone blinked an eye until the principal who, in the last term of his second year, found out what had been going on, and had an apoplexy. FJ wasn't overly fussed because he was approaching the end of his two years of country service, and he was due for a transfer.

1973: Pre-ordained destiny? (Marnie's words, not FJ's) In 1973, having completed his country service, FJ was transferred to in Cabramatta, in Sydney's south-western suburbs. It was only twenty minutes away from his home, so he found himself living back with his parents. That was another challenge entirely. After two years of choosing his own adventure, fitting back into the family house-rules wasn't easy. A huge complication was the fact that Marnie lived nearby, and they visited each other's homes regularly. The relationship had 'progressed' (don't ask!). They set a wedding date for the May school holidays, and began making the arrangements. It all took on a surreal aspect for FJ. His idea of married life was based on his own parents who had a life-long loving, sharing relationship. Marnie's father had died from a debilitating wartime injury so there wasn't much to learn there.

The wedding was a comparatively small affair by today's standards. The reception was held in the barn-style shed in an outer suburban property of one of Marnie's sisters and they honeymooned at Jenolan Caves. On Their return they lived briefly at her mother's house, then house-sat her brother's house for six weeks while he was away. They tried looking for suitable rented accommodation without success and finally, and very fortunately, were able to buy a new, but very plain home unit in Cabramatta where they lived for just six months, while Marnie completed her Arts degree.

1974: Pre-ordained fatality? (FJ's words, not Marnie's) Their world was turned upside-down early in 1974 when Marnie realised she had not enrolled in the Diploma of Education course at the University of NSW for that year. The only placement she could find was at Newcastle University. It was the beginning of a slide into an abyss. FJ had to apply for a compassionate transfer to Newcastle which he was lucky enough to get, in early in March.

They stayed with a good friend for a couple of weeks while Marnie searched for, and eventually managed to find, a flat. FJ was working full time, so wasn't much help. He was settling into his fourth school in four years, trying to pay the rent and a mortgage on their home unit and adjusting being first-year newlyweds.

For Marnie, in the 1970s the move away from family and friends and her attendance at the University of Newcastle opened an array of opportunities, including an active interest in women's liberation, which later led to involvement in Women's Electoral Lobby.

She abandoned a school teaching career, the very reason for the move to Newcastle, in favour of working in the Health Department in Newcastle and later pursuing an academic career. Among other things, FJ had badly misjudged Marnie's ambitions. (It was that of Cressida in Shakespeare's *Troilus and Cressida,* often described as, 'false Cressida, a paragon of female inconstancy'.

On 26th May 1974, a little over a year since their marriage, the Norwegian bulk carrier, the *Sygna*, ran aground on Newcastle Beach. That date signifies the beginning of the end of his marriage.

It was then that Marnie attended a Saturday night party given at a Watt Street, Newcastle Hospital staff residence with her older sister. The Signa was wrecked in one night. Their marriage took three months.

The end came when FJ was asked by a mate to accompany him to Canberra one weekend. They returned home unexpectedly early for FJ to discover that Marnie had invited another man to stay the night.

She had broached the subject of sexual relationships and had brought home a couple of books: *The Harrad Experiment* is a fictional novel by Robert H Rimmer which is written, as if it is the report of a real experiment, in which a group of college students are assigned opposite sex roommates; exercise and play sports in the nude and are expected to have multiple sex partners. The other book was Henry Miller's *Sexus*, in which the main character recounts his searing fictionalized sexual escapades in graphic detail. I had obviously been asleep at the marriage wheel.

When I confronted her she resented my interference. She had redefined our marriage arrangements. Three days later she walked out. Our marriage came to an end sixteen months after its commencement. Forty years later he discovered Marnie had told family members, and others, we'd had an 'open relationship'. In very recent years she referred to herself then as, 'young and immature' and that, in her own words, she was escaping, *'our pre-ordained trajectory'.*

When FJ read her comment, he could only think, 'If that trajectory had been pre-ordained, it should have been aborted before take-off!'

FJ never understood what went wrong. The number seven has astrological significance if one believes that sort of thing. All he could do was accept what happened as fact and admit that the chosen seven-year period was a life-changing one.

Infidelity leaves an irremovable scar.

Regarding adversity, the philosophical attitude of the Stoics to events in our lives, is sometimes summarised as: *It's not what happens in life. It's how you deal with it.*

The Stoics had virtue as their primary guiding principle.

FJ couldn't remember anyone talking about virtue in the 1970s.

Charles Dickens summed up these seven years of his life perfectly:

*"It was the best of times, it was the worst of times, it was the age of wisdom, it was the age of foolishness, it was the epoch of belief, it was the epoch of incredulity, it was the season of light, it was the season of darkness, it was the spring of hope, **it was the winter of despair."***

First Female Phalaropes

George Haith

There are about ten thousand bird species in the world and with the options now available for international travel, it is possible to see a significant proportion of them. Many birds in the tropics have spectacular colouring and behaviours, notably Birds of Paradise through to Humming Birds with many in between. These were the stuff of seemingly impossible dreams when growing up in England during the 1950s, the local 'exotics' being a pink Jay and a black and white migratory Smew duck, both with conventional bird profiles. As a child, I had mulled over a European Bird Guide and was aware that birds come in all shapes and colours. I was particularly struck by the images of the Phalarope family (Grey, Red-necked and, a rare vagrant to Western Europe, Wilson's). They captured my imagination because of their small size, delicate build and spectacular breeding plumage. Although they breed in the northern latitudes, two of them also spend the winter out at sea as they don't just wade but can also swim, aided by their unusual lobed feet. However, of the three, it was love at first sight for the Wilson's Phalarope; 'elegant' isn't a word usually associated with birds but for this species, it fits.

What is more, Phalaropes have evolved a neat technique for obtaining food while floating in shallow water, pirouetting with their feet down, stirring up the mud. They take food items that float to the surface using, in the case of Wilson's, an amazing needle-like bill. Add a slender neck with its dramatic contrasting plumage and it's an image once seen, never forgotten. These birds, theoretically, were in my reach. However, in the years after scanning the bird guide, I had been singularly unsuccessful at finding them. Given their preferred breeding habitat of exposed moorlands with extensive pools of water, trying to find them was hard yakka. Six weeks in Scotland and the Shetland Islands drew a blank. Four weeks trekking in severe conditions in Iceland had turned up Harlequin ducks, King Eider and Gyrfalcons, all impressive birds but not a sign of these illusive waders. My one consolation had been a Grey Phalarope, sex unknown in its bland winter plumage, on a small pond behind a freezing windswept sea wall on the Kentish coast.

Trying to find a rare vagrant like the Wilson's Phalarope might seem Quixotic but like gamblers anywhere, if you have a 'win' there is an assumption another could be close. In my case I found an equally rare vagrant in the form of a smaller wader, a White-rumped Sandpiper. Another North American species, it had been blown 5-6,000kms off course and arrived at a wetland just up the road from the bird observatory where I was staying. Stalking that bird to get a good view took a while, crawling through long grasses and thistles to get over an embankment. There was real satisfaction in not disturbing the bird but it was, after all, just another small brown wader, the rump only visible when it flew off, stage left, of its own accord. No 'wow' factor with that one.

In later years, trips to the USA, Africa and Australia resulted in seeing many spectacular birds, their number boosted when we emigrated here 30 years ago. Whether it was tiny, vividly-coloured field wrens, spectacular parrots or majestic albatross, they all had their virtues but only one could be classed, at a stretch, as elegant. It was the Australian Bustard, a large bird, sometimes described as 'stately' though 'imperious' might be nearer the mark, given the lofty disdain it appears to have for human visitors. Boat trips out to the Continental Shelf offered the prospect of Light-mantled Sooty Albatross; elegance personified for these precision flying duos but the odds were low and 'twas not to be. That first love, the Wilson's Phalarope remained in the memory banks and seemed destined to stay there.

One of the joys of travel is encounters with wildlife in the most unexpected places. There often seems to be a degree of reverse psychology, given the amazing number of times something special is seen, without binoculars or a camera to hand. When driving, there can be fleeting glimpses of sought-after species but safety dictates that no matter what the temptation, eyes stay on the road, there is no sudden braking and the steering wheel doesn't move. Consequently, in a car, the chance of seeing something special with the naked eye, and with the time to appreciate it, is almost non-existent. Almost.

We were on a touring holiday in the Rocky Mountains, staying in Vernal, Utah, 200kms east of Salt Lake City. It was a convenient stop-over between the Arches National Park and Yellowstone, with the advantage of access to the Dinosaur National Monument and its spectacular Quarry Museum, plus one of the national wildlife refuges. A few easy days were also welcome having just reached the literal high point of the trip at 9,000ft when driving over the Argyle Ridge in the Ashley National Forest.

As we drove out to the Ouray Refuge, I was not optimistic that we would see much, mid-morning, given the season was dry and in mid-May, most of the migrating birds were well north on their breeding grounds. However, the map showed wetlands to our right beside the approach road to the refuge so it was eyes-peeled as we came up to that sector. Two pairs of eyes are better than one and while my passenger isn't as keen on birds as I am, she has derived some satisfaction over the years, acting as a 'spotter', conjuring-up sought-after species with uncanny regularity.

The wetlands marked on the map turned out to be inaccessible, but the road at this point was elevated several metres above the paddocks to our left. One of these, ahead of us, had a fifty square metre puddle of water at the base of the embankment, and, I was informed reliably, was full of birds at that. The gods smiled, there was no traffic, so I could drift the car across to the hard shoulder overlooking the pool. I subsequently recorded over fifty birds there from thirteen species but before I had even got the binoculars out, it was apparent that these included several phalaropes. Just as art historians can look at a painting purported to be by an old master and say, 'it feels right', so for birdwatchers there is the concept of 'jizz', the barely definable features which can identify a bird. Even with the naked eye, the jizz said there were phalaropes there.

Frantic fumbling while grabbing the binoculars off the back seat seemed to take an age, with my left shoulder threatening dislocation, all the while looking through the passenger window and praying the birds would stay put. There was another anxious moment with the noise from the drive motor as my wife's window went down. I adjusted the focus screw and there they were. As if laid out on a platter, I had eight Wilson's in full breeding plumage, the most beautiful phalarope of the three, all of which are unusual as the female is more brightly coloured than the male. She is also larger and has a neat line in role reversal, initiating the courting process, defending her mate and the nest area before leaving him to incubate the eggs while she takes an early mark and migrates south.

The migration of these dainty birds, 23cm long and weighing only seventy grams, takes them from breeding grounds in the north down to Argentina using salt-rich waterways along the way without, in their case, going out to sea. Many are seen on the Great Salt Lake but Vernal is in the Green River valley, providing an alternative route east of the Wasatch Mountains for some of the population.

Here, I was above them at close range with the car acting as an effective hide so I could watch them perform; wading, swimming and feeding among the less interesting species. To say I drooled over these birds wouldn't go far enough. 'Struck dumb' didn't apply either as I couldn't stop talking about them, both to myself and my long-suffering wife. I heard a suggestion that my emotional compass needed recalibration. My excuse was simply that after fifty-five years, this was a dream come true; which was accepted with resigned good grace, happy to see a lifetime ambition of mine fulfilled. Ten minutes stoking the memory banks and then a quiet getaway without disturbing the birds. The refuge itself was a bit of a fizzer apart from the stiff-legged gait of a rapidly departing bear, so another ogle of the Wilson's was in order on our return trip.

As I clock-up the years, I seem to find connections in what could otherwise be seen as random events. Sometimes expressed by the six degrees of separation principle, we are all somehow linked. With the benefit of hindsight, the next momentous sightings should have been no surprise. In our journey north into the wilds of Montana, we toured another refuge, but drew a blank on more phalaropes. There were waders, including one which seemed to me to have an odd posture, previously only seen in an illustration by the USA's great nineteenth century bird artist, James Audubon. In my ignorance, I assumed the artist had got it wrong, a hangover from earlier years when artists worked from stuffed specimens and had to guess what they looked like in the wild. Reality, in my case, was a salutary experience. However, the standout wader there, metaphorically, was another elegant species, the Upland Sandpiper, formerly known as Bartram's Sandpiper. Thanks to a well-thumbed USA Bird Guide, it was instantly recognisable as it emerged from the grasses onto the gravel exit road, disappearing from sight below the bonnet as I braked to a standstill. I reversed cautiously and dragged the binoculars up, praying it hadn't budged. Recognizable because of its long legs, slender neck and poise, its mottled light brown plumage was excellent camouflage. However, it couldn't hold a candle to the Wilson's, not that I was complaining after another magical encounter, with my lucky charm beside me in the passenger seat. Later research showed a tenuous linkage.

Given how special the Wilson's Phalarope is, it begs the question of who was Alexander Wilson? Born in Scotland in 1766, he moved to Pennsylvania in 1794 and worked as a teacher before meeting the leading US ornithologist of the day, William Bartram. Bartram encouraged Wilson in the study of birds, especially their illustration, to such good effect that in later life, he became that nation's leading figure in the field. The life-like poses used for his bird compositions, unusual for that era in the USA, in turn may have inspired

James Audubon. Wilson produced a nine-volume definitive work on American ornithology, the last volume completed by a friend after Wilson's death in 1813. Of the two-hundred and fifty plus species Wilson illustrated, over ten percent were newly described and he named the elegant sandpiper in Bartram's honour. Wilson himself had five other birds named after him, including the Wilson's Petrel, another tiny bird which survives on the oceans but I'd guess he was mighty chuffed to have that phalarope on his epitaph. What a bird!

One of Life's Experiences

Pat Allen

We'd been married just five years and had moved into our new home, in a new suburb. I thought to engage with my kind and helpful neighbours. Everyone had been friendly and welcoming to us. Most were either of our age or a little older.

One couple was very old, the gentleman so frail from being gassed in World War I when he'd served as a doctor in the north of France. His lungs were severely affected and he found it necessary to wear a lambswool vest against his skin, whatever the weather. He was always gracious, though often not well, but he tried to be active daily. Everyone loved this humble and gentle man.

His wife, Yvonne, was very British, and soon we were to learn that she was a most frightful snob, such as we'd never met. However, she was glad to know that we were young and healthy neighbours and fancied that she could and would call upon us whenever necessary.

Her older sister, Doris, lived with them. Doris was a retired Christian missionary nurse home from South America, ever gentle and considerate, and not at all like her younger sibling. Doris became another much loved and respected neighbour.

Over the ensuing months, Yvonne set out to impress us.

"I was amongst the very first travellers allowed to enter the USSR after it was possible to get behind the Iron Curtain."

She was widely travelled and highly educated. A university degree was necessary if one was to be her close friend, and not just one of the servant class.

"This is the St Catherine's school that I started ... for daughters of nobility." She showed me a photo of the exclusive girls' school she had founded in Dorset and had been head mistress there till just 10 years ago, when she became the second wife of the doctor.

When showing me a photo of the village church she commented; "When our girls arrived for Sunday matins that main door was not an entrance for tradesmen." She smirked at a memory. "Even the local jeweller thought he could enter there, but we soon clarified that that was not so!"

Yvonne was proud of her antique furniture, object d'art, her long hair and a wardrobe of what once were expensive cocktail gowns, though it was all rather shabby by prevailing standards.

"We had cocktail parties almost weekly. Most useful for keeping in touch."

I was too embarrassed to comment. "My Georgian silver salver and serving spoons are rare," she said. "They are irreplaceable and very valuable."

Their large garden needed constant attention so to have a gardener work there two days a week was another proud boast.

"Mr Phillips will prune the blossom and the fruit trees when he comes to weed, and to mow the lawns on Thursday." The large block had extensive lawns. "I'm thinking we might have a garden party next Spring. We have the space. I'll have a caterer come to do for us."

One afternoon the phone rang with Yvonne asking would my husband, Keith please go over to them. She sounded a little anxious.

When he arrived, Yvonne, greeted him at the door.

"Come in," she commanded. "I think the doctor's dead."

On entering the cosy lounge room, he found the doctor certainly was dead sitting in his lounge chair, with a blanket covering his knees. He had died during his afternoon nap.

"I've rung our GP. He should be here soon."

Yvonne was dry-eyed and indicated that Keith should take a seat and wait with her. Then she clapped her hands quite briskly and called to Doris.

"We'll have tea now." This was how she had ordered her servants when in England.

Doris obeyed, producing a tray with English breakfast tea and some cucumber sandwiches, no matter the hour.

So, along with the deceased doctor in his chair, they sat, sipped tea, and chatted about the doings of the day.

Soon the visiting doctor arrived and all necessary matters were dealt with. Keith stayed with Yvonne and Doris till the undertaker had arrived and removed the deceased doctor. He helped the ladies to restore the lounge room and then returned to me to relate all that had happened. Both of us were greatly upset by his death.

"I'll phone and let them know that I will do a meal for them."

There was great relief in Yvonne's voice over the phone. I would not describe it as gratitude as she seemed to have expected such help. I set about preparing food. By 6 pm when all was ready, I set a tray with a fresh cloth, and covered plates of hot food for Keith to deliver to them.

When he returned, I could not fail to see that he was chuckling. He related that Yvonne welcomed the meal, then suddenly realised that her false teeth were on the coffee table and she had no way to eat it. He smiled as he described her embarrassment as she grabbed for her teeth.

"You didn't see that, did you?" she'd spluttered. Her air of superiority crumpled at this exposure. He was able to soothe her discomfiture.

"See what?" he had replied.

We assisted them with preparations for the funeral. I cooked and served suitable finger foods for the wake which was held at their home. Doris was vocal in her appreciation and Yvonne nodded her approval. For Yvonne, humility, grace and appreciation was not readily displayed.

Despite Yvonne's faults, we remained her friendly and helpful neighbours, though no longer naive ones, till both she and Doris died within the following few years.

Johnny's

Lorraine James

"Right – I understand. Well – that's a pity. Lillian won't be happy but I'll explain your rules. Thanks Jack."

Dad hung up.

I was hovering in the hallway outside the living room, fingers and arms crossed. I would have crossed my legs as well had the left one not been encumbered by a heavy white plaster with a wooden rocker attached to the bottom.

I hobbled back into my bedroom and sat on the edge of my bed in total despair. My beautiful dress hung optimistically on the wardrobe door handle.

"Forget it," I said to it. I was crying of course. Who wouldn't after such devastating news. The prospect – the totally humiliating experience that lay ahead of me – reared up in my imagination.

I stared at the dress – a beautiful fifties number in blue and green tartan taffeta – ballerina skirt, stiffened petticoats and an extravagant emerald green sash. Through my tears it appeared to wobble about in watery sympathy.

Dad appeared at the door.

"Well Lil. It's bad news I'm afraid. I've just talked to Jack Bolton and ..."

"I know! I heard *everything!*" I yelled, dramatically throwing myself back onto the bed, aiming for the pillows face down as I had seen in the movies. That was a flop. I just sort of rolled onto my left side anchored by the weight of the plaster. I lay there and stared up at Dad and sobbed "I can't go. I just can't. It would be too embarrassing."

Dad regarded me impassively. "Buck up Lil" he said. "Get a grip. It's not the end of the world," and he ambled off.

In my small world back in the early 1950's Johnny's was the dream beginning of a teenager's social life. At fourteen years of age all the girls in my set had been hanging out for this moment for ever. Johnny's was *the* ballroom dancing school that everyone aspired to. Separated by our education in an exclusively girls' school, this was our big chance to meet boys.

My school group, sitting on the lawn in the hedged sanctuary at lunchtime, had been enjoying weeks of speculation about the pending first night at Johnny's. What we were going to wear was an important point of discussion and whether our fathers would allow us to wear lipstick (Tanjee Natural of course) and nylon stockings.

For me, all this happy anticipation had been stymied by an event in the gymnasium. Resplendent in the ugly white blouses we always wore above our equally ugly pleated skirts, on this day our bottom halves sported voluminous black exercise bloomers and sandshoes. Lined up in four teams of six the brief was that we were to climb to the top of the wall bars, touch a marker at the very top, climb down like monkeys and run to the back of our line while the next girl repeated the performance. My turn. I climbed nimbly to the top, touched the marker and on my way down thought 'I'll jump.' I did and landed in a heap, my left foot shooting excruciating pains up my leg.

After school I took the bus as usual and hobbled the half mile home. Mum took a look at my foot which was swelling fast and drove me to the hospital where it was declared 'a fracture' and the plaster applied.

Under normal circumstances I would have just resigned myself to six weeks of healing but all I could think of was Johnny's which was what led to Dad's phone call with the owner Jack Bolton. Dad knew him of course. Dad knew everybody. And Jack had said to Dad, once my plight had been explained, that he didn't have any time for students who didn't turn up on the first night. "Lillian can just sit and watch" he said to Dad. "That way she'll still be learning."

Having left my crutches at home I hobbled into Johnny's Dance Studio on the first night and joined the other girls sitting lined up along the wall on one side of the room. I hastily covered my plaster with my copious skirt. On the other side of the hall boys were also lined up. All from private schools they were wearing their formal black suits and uncomfortable stiff white collars which they kept trying to adjust by shoving a finger down inside them and moving their necks back and forth. They all looked about twelve. They all appeared to be perspiring.

Jack Bolton walked into the centre of the room, clapped his hands and after a welcoming speech said "Now, for starters we're going to learn The Waltz. Gentlemen – take a partner." The boys stood up, awkwardly shuffling their feet around. Nobody crossed the floor.

"Get moving!" shouted Mr. Bolton. "Don't be wimps." So, like a herd of frightened deer, boys advanced on us. They all looked terribly short.

I sat there absolutely shaking with fear. What if no-one chose me? That was the worst fear of all – to be a wallflower.

But a boy was standing in front of me with his hand out. "You from St Cuths?" It was a statement rather than a question. The St Cuthbert's Girls School uniform was a navy and blue tartan.

"No" I replied. "I'm at EGGS." That was Ellerton Girls' Grammar School.

"Okay" he said. "Wanna dance?"

I looked up at him and lifted my skirt to reveal the rocker with a line of frozen toes displayed. On my working foot I wore a silver dance shoe.

"I can't dance" I whimpered. "I broke my foot."

My potential partner looked totally brassed off and immediately started to look around for another target.

"C'mon Girl! Get up." An immaculate man with slick blond hair had appeared. I was terrified. This, I just knew, was the notorious Mr. Stoll. His reputation preceded him, that is, strict and scary. All potential students had heard about Mr. Stoll.

In our imaginations he was the equivalent of a member of the SS, World War II still featuring prominently in our history and geography curriculums.

"I can't." I stuttered, lifting my skirt higher to show him the plaster.

"For heavens' sake, then why did you come?" He was seriously irritated.

I was determined not to cry so responded defiantly. "Because Mr. Bolton told me to."

For the next four weeks I sat meekly in front of the wallflower wall and observed, and then one wonderful day the plaster was removed and my dancing days began.

As a reward for turning up Mr. Bolton arranged for me to take private lessons free of charge so I could catch up. But my current losing streak appeared to continue. My personal coach was to be Mr. Stoll. But boy! the positive result of this absolute downer was that, despite the fear, Mr. Stoll turned me into a pretty good ballroom dancer ... if I say so myself.

My First Numbats

George Haith

For anyone interested in seeing Australian native animals in daylight, they arguably come in one general shape and colour but with a range of sizes, from bandicoots up through bettongs and into the wallabies and kangaroos. We managed to find several species across this size range over the years, including Brown Bandicoots literally at the bottom of the garden. Fifteen years in Tasmania included frequent sightings of platypus at our local arboretum in the north west of the state, including classic 'swim-unders' as we stood on low wooden bridges. Tiger quolls and Tasmanian devils were fluked in daylight and echidnas were familiar beasts from trips across the eastern states. However, while all of these species are special, one marsupial, the numbat, (aka Banded Anteater) captures the imagination like no other, using all four legs for motion and with a unique combination of colour, profile and habit. They are, quite simply, spectacular.

Seeing one proved to be a major challenge. Formerly widespread in southern Australia from the West coast across just into Victoria, their range has contracted over the last 200 years due to land clearance and predation by introduced cats and foxes. So much so that the wild population is now confined to a small area of Western Australia (WA). Finding them on a trip to WA would be a lottery but fortunately, pioneering work by Dr John Wamsley in South Australia resulted in translocation of some of these iconic animals to a 50 square kilometre reserve established in the Mallee in 1989. It wasn't a conventional reserve as this one had a feral-proof fence and no cats, foxes or goats for that matter, all essential prerequisites for successful native mammal breeding programmes. Four other reintroduced species were also in residence in smaller controlled areas of the reserve but numbats were the only ones amenable to daylight viewing.

Weighing-in at 4-500 grams and with a body length up to 27 cm, these beautifully marked carnivorous marsupials are the only representative of their family. Imagine a heavily-furred meercat with a bandicoot's head and grey/russet/black colouring. Add five or more vertical white stripes on the flanks and a pronounced horizontal black line along the pale side of the head through the eye. With a tail almost the length of the body, the overall effect puts it near the top of the cuteness scale. Feeding almost exclusively on termites, they are not strong enough to raid established mounds but concentrate instead on the shallow termite runways leading to the nest. Given that termites are mainly active in temperatures above twenty-four degrees, numbats sleep during the night and come out to feed when the temperature gets the termites on the move.

Keen to support the conservation efforts for this species, we became 'friends' of the reserve and made trips to the mainland to participate in working bees. A weekend working deep in the Mallee of South Australia proved to be hard yakka, contending with flies and heat even in winter. The first trip was spent repainting the accommodation units and assisting with other general maintenance. We saw the nocturnal marsupials on spot-lighting trips to top up their food and water but the chances of seeing numbats around the buildings were slim and they remained on our 'wish list'. Undaunted, we returned the following year to be tasked with pulling Ward's Weed, an invasive species, and bailing-out a pond near the residential buildings to repair the liner.

After dark, we entered the burrowing bettong enclosure in order to feed and count them; an interesting exercise with 30+ marsupials demonstrating the finer points of chaos theory. This area was also home to cages for Stick-nest Rats, which had to be fed with salt bush and have their water topped-up, all monitored by a very pale Boobook Owl, waiting in a nearby tree for the one-that-got-away. Our last stop for the night was the adjacent bilby enclosure. These are 'diggers' par excellence, turning-over enormous quantities of soil searching for food and creating burrows up to three metres long and one and a half metres deep. Their area resembled a hectare of minefield so we took care to stay on the chook-wire walkway while the bilbies zoomed around the new bollards moving through their temporary home.

Seeing these iconic Australian animals was a real thrill, the stuff that dreams are made of given that their plight is almost as dire as the numbat's. However, big pointy ears aside, they are little different from the bettongs so are way below numbats on the cuteness scale. Hopefully having demonstrated our commitment to the cause, I asked the working-bee team leader if there was any way we could improve our chances of seeing numbats. As luck would have it, a scientist from Brisbane was in residence, working on numbat ecology for her PhD. A plea-bargain was struck, so provided we made an early start, this good lady would spare us a couple of hours to guide us to an active burrow.

On the following morning at 6 am, we were driven out with our radio-tracker guide to monitor one of the numbat families in the main feral-proof enclosure, an expanse of over a thousand hectares. Under a cloudless sky, we were dropped-off in a fairly open area of grassy understorey with isolated shrubs up to two-metres high. This was surrounded by taller, multi-stemmed Mallee trees, their bark positively glowing in the low-angled light. There was also the incongruous sight of three dark green plastic chairs, side-by-side, apparently only a few metres away from an occupied burrow, confirmed by suitable 'pings' on the tracking system. The rules, explained before we left the vehicle, were simple. No movement and no sound, or we could blow our chance and ruin the morning for our guide and any volunteers to follow. Piece of cake surely, I thought.

The first motionless half hour was straightforward but then as it warmed-up, birds started to fly by. These included a Mallee special, the Purple-crowned Lorikeet, three birds giving their high-pitched 'tziet' call so I had to resist the instinct to raise my binoculars. By 8am, treecreepers were calling in the distance and flies were doing unspeakable things to our faces so I was desperate to scratch my nose. The tension was palpable as I risked a prolonged blink but fortunately, I was looking when a clump of grass in front of me morphed into an adult female numbat. She treated us to a broadside of seven white stripes, did a ninety-degree turn and was gone after all of five seconds. At last! The real thing after thousands of kilometres, multiple photos and stuffed specimens; my initial elation tempered by a slightly rueful, "is that it?"

Our guide didn't move a muscle, we all stayed put and the tension built up as the minutes passed. Then there were sudden intakes of breath and at least one dropped jaw across the three chairs. A small pointed snout came straight towards us, stopping four metres away as a two-thirds size juvenile came out to warm-up in the sun. It was joined by a second one, more wary this time, standing on all-fours and poised for flight. They were perfectly marked, simply gorgeous but horribly exposed to avian predators while they charged their batteries. After a few minutes, the first one turned and extended its tongue, a livid orange-red, 3 cm party popper, while the other one blinked a few times before following suit. It was as if this was a special performance, just for our benefit. They then rocked forward and extended their forelegs in cat-like full body stretches before vanishing into the scrub, not to be seen again.

Ten minutes of Mallee magic and not a dry eye between the three of us, all initially speechless. I felt incredibly privileged to have witnessed this display. Our guide had never seen it before and was thrilled on her own account, while also delighted for us that our discipline had paid off. As for me, after fifty years of wildlife watching on five continents, this was up in my top five viewing experiences, made all the more memorable by being only the second of these shared with my better-half. We strolled (swaggered?) the two kilometres back to the base, taking nesting Little Eagles in our stride. Normally, as a life-long birdwatcher, this would have been a sight of wonder, but in our post-numbat-experience world, it was relegated to a simple "oh, great".

The other volunteers were already hard at work weeding around the Mallee fowl enclosure where we would join them shortly. Meanwhile, over a late breakfast on the veranda and discussing all things numbat, we watched Scrub Robins and White-eared Honeyeaters fly down to the bushes before christening the re-lined pond around the corner of the building. A while later, returning from a trip to the facilities conveniently located nearby, I was stunned to see my second adult numbat, drinking from the pond! Our guide and the site manager were off like scalded cats, trying to keep tabs on this errant beast which wasn't known to be in the area. My own initial reaction, after recovering from the surprise, was that I could have slept-in after all! However, as someone once said, you can only appreciate a music concert properly when you have queued in the rain for the tickets. After days of volunteering and an anxious hour in the Mallee waiting for numbats, I know what they meant.

As for the numbats, the breeding programme was successful, resulting in their reintroduction to an even larger feral-free reserve in NSW. The pioneering work of John Wamsley was continued by the late Martin Copley who founded the Australian Wildlife Conservancy (AWC) thirty years ago. This organisation, alone and in partnership, has gone on to create additional large feral-free zones, including ones in WA and the Northern Territory plus two under contract to the NSW National Parks and Wildlife Service in The Pilliga and at Mallee Cliffs. The feral free zone at the latter covers over nine-thousand hectares, representing sixteen percent of the total park area. Numbats, bilbies and two other long-lost marsupials were reintroduced there within two years of completion of the fence with more to follow. AWC research on control of cat and fox populations 'outside the fence' continues with the hope that one day, my grandsons' generation may be able to see numbats and other small marsupials as a matter of course.

Tone, a
Musical Memoir

John Franks

"With tone, people will listen to almost anything;
without it, no one wants to hear you
play anything." (Clive Amadio)

During a memorable music lecture while attending Westmead Teachers' College in 1969, I was offered and accepted the loan of a clarinet. I'd never even touched one before and knew nothing about how to play it, but I'd been smitten by the silky-smooth tones of Acka Bilk playing *Stranger on the Shore* and I was hooked. The question was, 'how do I learn to play it?'

I tried tutor books: *A Tune a Day* parts I and II, and made minimal progress but, like a fisherman who gets a few nibbles every now and then, I persisted.

Five years later, with the borrowed clarinet left behind at College, I found myself passing Music Headquarters in New Lambton, where I saw a clarinet for sale. I almost salivated when I saw it and on impulse, went into the shop and asked to try it. One thing was made clear that day: I was still in love with the idea of playing clarinet.

To improve my playing, I had a few lessons from a trumpet playing friend, which mostly focused on learning to read music and acquiring the basics. Later that year, I approached my school principal with the idea of starting up a school band. That led to contact with Education Department Music Adviser, Tom Naisby, and the Newcastle Conservatorium of Music and in particular, Clive Amadio, the clarinet teacher – professor would be a better word.

I admit I fell under the spell of that great musician. Briefly, Clive Amadio, AM was an honorary life member of the Clarinet Society of New South Wales. He was a guru (if mostly a self-publicising one) on clarinet and saxophone, and confidante of Sir Eugene Goossens, the first permanent conductor of the Sydney Symphony Orchestra.

Clive had presented his own music programme, *From Me to You,* on ABC radio from 1939-1958. Under his leadership, the Clive Amadio Quintet was given prime Sunday night listening time on ABC 2BL, now 702AM.

FROM ME TO YOU
The Life & Times of
CLIVE AMADIO

Donald Westlake

Clive was a source of inspiration and perspiration. He was fanatical about tone production. His core principle was that of the opening quote above: "With tone, people will *listen* to almost anything but without it, no one wants to *hear* you play anything."

In 1980, I successfully auditioned for a place in the City of Newcastle Concert Band (CNCB). Some years later, I was awarded Life Membership. Concert bands have all the wind instruments of an orchestra but no stringed instruments. Auditioning for a Conservatorium scholarship, a position in a band or orchestra, or even a role in a play, is a nerve-wracking experience. I've done all three. By far the worst in that area is sitting for Australian Music Examinations Board grade exams, especially when one is nearing forty and the next kid in the queue doing the same exam is fifteen. The band was later renamed the City of Newcastle Wind Orchestra, and eventually came under the auspices of UON as The University of Newcastle Wind Orchestra. Under Ian Cook, it attracted both academic staff and advanced students from 'The Con', the Conservatorium of Music, as well as local instrumentalists.

I had the good fortune to have made a long-term friend in the band-cum-orchestra. Our connection went back to our school band days. John (Spike) Roddenby and I had sat next to each other at rehearsals and performances for almost twenty years, and when the time came to leave the orchestra we continued our own rehearsals independently. We'd both been students of Clive Amadio and often, when we struck problems, we would look at each other, laugh, and say, "What would Clive say?" It was more than enough to make us put our heads down and work.

In 1998 Donald Westlake, former principal clarinettist with the Sydney Symphony Orchestra, interviewed me for his book, From Me to You, The Life and Times of Clive Amadio (1999). Westlake asked if he could quote parts of the conversations I'd had with Clive. When I asked why, he said, "You seem to have had a very good relationship with him."

That relationship included some rather risqué descriptions of wannabe musicians: "They spent too much time on the pink oboe." Clive would say. He also described the embouchure – the way in which the clarinet is sealed in the mouth to direct the flow of air onto the reed by saying, "A sphincter provides the perfect seal – hopefully!".

I will never forget the first lesson with Clive. After initial introductions he asked me to play something on my new made-in-France Selmer (Series 10) clarinet. No sooner had I made a sound than he told me to stop. He then proceeded to put his hands on my face and shape my cheeks and embouchure which, he asserted, would help provide the best tone. I didn't know what to think when he placed his hands on my face. It's not something any man except my father had ever done. Once that initial shock passed, I realised I had to trust the man if I was going to get the full benefit of his tuition. His inspiration guided me through several Australian Music Examinations Board (AMEB) grade exams and when he left, I carried on to Grade 7 before going to university at age forty. I was a slow learner.

Learning is inevitably a process of self-improvement and hopefully, personal growth. What matters most is what we do with the new knowledge and the analysis of subsequent actions.

That day I bought my first clarinet was full of lessons. I learnt another during my pre-purchase test when a stray dog ran up the street to the door of the shop and started howling. I learnt that everyone is a critic, not only the humans, and that includes us – especially me.

Source unknown, but I thank whoever first thought of it and all of those who have shared it since.

Natural Highs

Some things can be done a million times, but still give the same buzz as if it was the first. Remember this and treat yourself and others to this type of smile. Add your natural highs on the next page to keep the joy of firsts continuing into the joy of seconds, thirds...

1. Falling in love.
2. Laughing so hard your face hurts.
3. A hot shower.
4. No lines at the supermarket.
5. A special glance.
6. Getting mail.
7. Taking a drive on a pretty road.
8. Hearing your favourite song on the radio.
9. Lying in bed listening to the rain outside.
10. Hot towels fresh out of the dryer.
11. Chocolate milkshake (or vanilla or strawberry).
12. A bubble bath.
13. Giggling.
14. The beach.

15. Finding a 20 dollar note in your coat from last winter.
16. Laughing at yourself.
17. Looking into their eyes and knowing they Love you.
18. Midnight phone calls that last for hours.
19. Running through sprinklers.
20. Laughing for absolutely no reason at all.
21. Having someone tell you that you're beautiful.
22. Laughing at an inside joke with friends.
23. Accidentally overhearing someone say something nice about you.
24. Waking up and realizing you still have a few hours left to sleep.
25. Your first kiss (either the very first or with a new partner).
26. Making new friends or spending time with old ones.
27. Playing with a new puppy.
28. Having someone play with your hair.
29. Sweet dreams.
30. Hot chocolate.
31. Road trips with friends.
32. Swinging on swings.
33. Making eye contact with a cute stranger.

34. Making chocolate chip cookies.
35. Having your friends send you homemade cookies.
36. Holding hands with someone you care about.
37. Running into an old friend and realizing that some things (good or bad) never change.
38. Watching the expression on someone's face as they open a much desired present from you.
39. Watching the sunrise.
40. Getting out of bed every morning and being grateful for another beautiful day.
41. Knowing that somebody misses you.
42. Getting a hug from someone you care about deeply.
43. Knowing you've done the right thing, no matter what other people think.

Our Authors

Black Crow Walking {Crow Woman, as named by the Lakota Ghosthorse Indians}
French Doors and Red Curls

Crow has trained and worked as a professional artist since her children grew up 20 years ago. She followed in her father's footsteps as an artist and eventually was a forerunner in painting with encaustic and cold wax in Australia. Since losing the use of her studio, she has turned her artistic talent to writing. She has two self-published books of poetry called Drifting Leaves and Captured Moments, published in 2019. The same year she also published her first non-fiction book, Angels Speak. Since then, she has been in two anthologies for Sapphic touch and Sapphic Flows and two for Poetry in the Pub. She is currently writing a non-fiction encyclopedia about spirituality and, for light relief, is rewriting Grimm's fairy tales. Her story of Rapunzel which appears in this anthology is one of those tales.

Bronwyn MacRitchie

Foiled

Bronwyn has been writing short stories since childhood. Upon retirement from music teaching, she began attending creative writing workshops with an interest in creative writing and memoir. In 2020, she published Pixie Dust, a memoir of her childhood and in 2021, during Covid lockdown, produced an audio version of her book. She is a member of both Hunter Writers and Lake Macquarie FAW and has been a frequent finalist in the Newcastle Herald Short Story Competition. Bronwyn is currently working on her next memoir.

Diana Souter

First Flight

Diana was born in Broken Hill and attended SCEGS Tamworth. She attended St Catherine's Waverley, UNE Armidale NSW, London College of Music and Slough Management College UK and UTS Sydney. She holds qualifications in Music, Primary School Teaching, Adult Education, and Human Resources Management. She has lived in Sydney, Melbourne and London and now Nelson Bay, combining careers of business with family. Diana was a candidate for the Federal Elections for the seat of Grayndler (now Anthony Albanese's) and in 1998 and was a delegate to the national women's Constitution Convention in Canberra. She has travelled widely visiting over 43 countries and has three adult children and three grandchildren. On moving to Nelson Bay in 2004 (supposedly to retire) she met and married Ron Souter (a singer) and in 2009 they established the first Community Choir in Port Stephens – the SeaSide Singers. as a writer, Diana has has had many short stories published in magazines including in the NSW Government Seniors stories of 2022. A copy of her recently published memoirs "From the Hill to the Bay" by Diana Bennett-Mills-Souter is in the South Australian Library of Genealogy.

Geoff Gibbson

A Friend
Oops

Geoff Gibbson is the pen name of one of the other authors in this publication, but if I told you about him, you would know who and his anonymity would no longer apply.

George Graves

More than a painting

George has been a member of the Lake Macquarie FAW for about ten years, writing short stories and some poems, mostly about people and relationships. Although they are largely fictional, he often draws on incidents from his past and incorporates these into the stories. George has a mathematics and electronic engineering background, so these have a very different style from that used in engineering journals where his name has appeared amongst the authors of various papers.

He loves reading about many different topics, including mathematics and quantum physics, but also often reads novels. George owns an old yacht and enjoys messing about in it on Lake Macquarie, where all the trivia of this world seems to fade away. He is particularly thankful for the encouragement he has received from members of the writing group to which he belongs.

George Haith
First Encounters with the Foreign Legion
First Female Phalaropes
My First Numbats

George trained as a scientist and spent a large part of his career writing technical reports. Now retired and with a life-long interest in natural history, he contributes wildlife commentaries to community-based organisations. He has also had four short stories published. His stories are born from his love of wildlife in Australia and abroad.

Jan Mitchell

Rewriting a Life

Jan retired from full-time English teaching in 1989 and retrained as a Natural Health Therapist. Since she retired to western Lake Macquarie, she has written five books. Her books can be purchased at Rathmines Post Office, Amazon, other booksellers or directly.

John Franks

Date Gone Wrong
The Place we Call Home
Pharaoh's Dream
Tone, A Musical Memoir

Avid teacher and researcher, John Franks has both bachelor's and master's degrees in education from the University of Newcastle (UON). After 40 years of primary school teaching, he dedicates much of his time to his other passions – the arts. In 2020, John's first book Memoirs (warts and all) of a Baby Boomer successfully sold out its first print run. His second book, Echoes, is a contemporary novel with a strong historical fiction element.

John's commitment to the Newcastle Theatre Company saw him awarded life-membership in 2011. John played for many years with the UON Wind Orchestra and currently conducts a small U3A orchestra in Lake Macquarie, New south Wales. John's story, *The Place We Call Home,* was published in the 2022 NSW Seniors Card Competition.

Judy Turner

The Red Coat

Judy Turner lives on the South Coast of New South Wales. Her stories have won awards and been short-listed in writing competitions and sixteen published to date. A collection of her short stories, titled Watermelon Days, is due for release early in 2023. Judy began writing in 2010 in order to record family stories. The Red Coat is a story of a true event.

Kate Mannell

Doorway to the Unknown

Kate graduated from an environmental sustainability degree in 2020. She is originally from Bathurst and has always loved writing. Travel writing is her favourite genre as she attempts to capture moments from her adventures to relive them again through words.
She was named Miss Maitland 2023.

Lorraine James

Mr Mitchell
Johnny's

Lorraine is a New Zealander living in Australia and has been a member of Southern Highland branch of The Fellowship of Australian Writers since 2019. She writes under two names: Kate Finn and Lorraine James.

Maggie Rose Carr

Shake up for a Rookie Cop
Struggle in the Darkness

Maggie relishes the world of fiction. An escape from the world of commitment and expectations. She has written sporadically throughout her life, both in her darkest hours and her happiest days. Her manuscripts include an assortment of many, many faded pages filled with scribbled ramblings. Most of them poems and anecdotes written for family and friends.

The realm of short stories now beckons. Diving in to explore its possibilities, she is hopeful that her offerings will be enjoyed by readers who share her journey. Maggie's stories in this anthology will be her firsts presented in published form.

Margaret Lock

The Locket

Margaret has enjoyed writing poems, short stories and articles since 1988. An inaugural member of Box Hill's The Aardvarkers' Poetry Group, she formed a small press publishing company with fellow writer, Gail Watson in 1992. From 2007-13, Margaret was secretary, occasional judge and competition co-ordinator for Peninsula FAW. After relocating to Northern Victoria, she became secretary of Murchison & District Historical Society. She enjoys writing and researching local and family history, and wrote *Sam's Meteorite* and *Space Gem: Mysteries of the Murchison Meteorite* for M&DHS. A member of Nagambie Lakes Writing Group, she enjoys developing stories for competitions.

Meg Boland

First Day in a New World

Meg married an Indonesian-Chinese student in the 1960s and loves to write about her travels.

Pat Allen

One of Life's Experiences

Pat Allen, a retired midwife, grandmother and avid scribbler, writes short stories and poetry, and seeks to record family history, memoirs and anecdotes passed down the generations. Pat is a past President of the Blue Mountains Writers branch of the Fellowship of Australian Writers. She has won awards, and been published in many anthologies and collections of short stories.

Pat Fern

Morgan Has His Turn
The Eye of the Needle

Pat is a versatile writer, exploring most genres. She likes fantasy, magic, spooky and ghost stories, and has written two about angelic intervention. She loves writing comedy – hearing people laugh makes her day. She also writes verse.

Pat is very English and much of her work is set in England. Pat says, "I can write factual articles if I have to but I love to let my imagination run free – if I can find it."

Patricia Ruell

The Strawberry Patch

Patricia has a PhD in Exercise and Sport Science and worked in a science research laboratory for many years. More recently Patricia joined a writer's group. Among several short stories she has published is The Rose-Print Dress, which won first prize in a Discovery Writers memoir competition. Patricia's story, The Strawberry Patch, was inspired by her first job weeding strawberries in the early 1970s.

Sandra Joy

The Pressure of a Name
That Night

Sandra Joy is a genre-hopper who writes in several genres and has a qualification that says she can. After publishing her first non-fiction book on helping others, she fell in love with the publishing industry and started her own business. Second to the publishing process, Sandra loves seeing the joy that others express when they see their first "Real Book".

Sandra has completed a Bachelor of Arts, majoring in English and Writing, and two minors in Education and Writing Studies. She has completed two courses from different universities on Editing and Publishing and is a member of several industry affiliations. In her spare time, she enjoys writing children's books, fiction and non-fiction stories, all under the mantra of Helping Words Matter.

Tony Lang

Forbidden Love
First News – Worse News!
My Worst ever Christmas Present
Rosemary's First Outing

Tony has always been interested in writing but wrote nothing until 1989 when *A Kangaroo Loose in the Top Paddock* appeared under the pseudonym Lachlan Ness.

Nothing followed for some years, until after living in Shetland and mainland Scotland formed *A Kangaroo Loose* trilogy. They were followed by *The Ness Fireside Book of God, Ghosts, Ghouls and other True Stories.* Later on, *What the Bible Really Says about Women* and a book of my poems, *The Channel Bank and other Verse* followed.

Waiting now for more inspiration!

Also available in the Life's Toolbox series:

PETS AND PESTS (2023)

What's in your toolbox? Your life experience has given you tools that can encourage, help, teach or humour others. Here, in the second of the series, is a collection of funny and enlightening stories about pets and pests. Join our authors on their journeys through their loves and frustrations, confusions and amusements, as they ascertain whether there really is a difference between pets and pests.

SILENT TRAIN WRECKS (2023)

What's in your toolbox? Your life experience has given you tools that can encourage, help, teach or humour others. Here, in the third of the series, is a collection of short stories about the weird, whacky and wonderful things travellers have seen and experienced on our train lines. Join our authors on their journeys through exposed relationships, fears and disasters, humorous and embarrassing situations, on our trains and platforms.

Submissions
open for:

TRUE

INSPIRED by truth

or FICTION

ADDICTIONS AND RECOVERY	AUSTRALIAN STORIES	MATURITY AND WISDOM
Encouraging stories about the experience and life during and after any type of addiction. Many are addicted to something, from drugs or alcohol, work or our mobile phones:	*Face it, Aussies are unique. But how? Let's explore our habits, histories and characteristics that make us truly Aussie (whatever that means).* *For example:*	*Like it or not, wisdom is supposed to come with age and experience. Let's hear about some of the valuable insight from those who have lived through more than us. Remember though:*
* Keep it purposeful—your story has the power to change a life! * Have a message that can help others. * The story does not have to be yours, does not have to identify the person, and does not have to be true,	* Aussie bravado * The good ol' BBQ. * Our environment and climate—from the beach to the fires, and what we do with it. * The hazards—our pot-holed roads and the creatures that bite.	* Maturity isn't always associated with age! * Your experience can help someone else when they go through the same thing. * Being older does not necessarily mean you are smarter.

https://kaniconsultants.com.au/submissions-open-2/

WHAT'S IN YOUR TOOLBOX?

Your life experience has given you tools that can encourage, help, teach, or humour readers. We want to share your story so readers:

Have a better day

Know they are not alone, and

Have tools to help themselves and others

Inspiration page:

Please use this space to record some of your firsts. I hope these stories and poems inspire you to try some more new experiences.

This is not the end of the journey for this book. Please make a note about it before passing it on to someone else. Let's see where these stories travel.

August 2023 - Sandra Boyd from Newcastle NSW wants to praise the authors! *(your turn)*

_____

_____

_____

_____

_____

_____

_____

www.ingramcontent.com/pod-product-compliance
Lightning Source LLC
Chambersburg PA
CBHW030619120726
47904CB00006B/1960